Unfinished Business

Michael Banister

Andrew Benzie Books
Walnut Creek, California

Published by Andrew Benzie Books
www.andrewbenziebooks.com

Printed in the United States of America

www.stolenidentitynovel.com

First Edition: November 2017

10 9 8 7 6 5 4 3 2 1

ISBN 978-1-941713-59-4

Thanks to my editors Kate McCracken, Bradley Francis and Linda Ross
Cover photo by Andrea Thrussell
Cover and book design by Andrew Benzie

I dedicate this novel to the victims of the unfolding calamity we see all around us, and I hope and pray for an end to the merciless materialism that has given rise to it.

TABLE OF CONTENTS

DRAMATIS PERSONAE

Danilo (AKA Dani and Cap'n Dante) and Dushan (AKA Dr. Dushansky)—stepbrothers.

Marta and Dimitri—Parents of Dushan, Aisha and Shimza ("the Younger"). Marta, from Slovenia, is the granddaughter of Shimza the Elder, AKA "Nonna". Dimitri fled Yugoslavia with baby Dushan after Marta's kidnapping during the breakup of Yugoslavia.

Adrijana—Dimitri's aunt who lives in Serbia.

Margaret—Dani's grandmother who lives in Liverpool.

Angus Ailshie—retired police inspector from Isle of Man who helped Dimitri find Marta.

Claude Prejean—the French Canadian engineer Dani rescued in a snowy Utah winter.

Carolyn Markos—Margaret's niece who kidnapped Dushan when he was five years old in Isle of Man.

Burt Sandor—Dani's late father, Carolyn's cousin and Margaret's son, who emigrated to San Francisco from Liverpool. He paid Carolyn to kidnap Dushan and sell him to Burt as a "replacement" for Burt's terminally son Markos.

Bulent Aksoy—the Bosnian criminal living in Liverpool who, in first book, convinced Carolyn and her colleague Derrick Nelson to participate in his organization's unofficial and illegal "adoption" scheme, a scheme that resulted in Carolyn's kidnapping of Dushan.

Goran Bolat—A former employee of Dimitri's fishing business in Belgrade. During the breakup of Yugoslavia, Goran joined the Yugoslavian army, kidnapped Marta and forced her to work as a nurse in an army camp.

Milan Vukadin, a Red Cross driver who, with Corporal Jovan Durkovic, rescued Marta and another prisoner, Seifullah Hamid, from Goran's army camp.

Charlotte Bekas—another niece of Margaret and second cousin of Burt's late wife Irene. She lives in New Jersey.

Makelle Ringhiero—Charlotte's nephew from San Francisco, an immigrant from Eritrea who grew up in a small town in California. He's a partner in a law firm on a sabbatical in Liverpool.

Jaelle Ringhiero—Makelle's daughter from a college flame, Heike.

Jaleh and Tom Kilpatrick—The couple first met Dimitri when he and Dushan arrived as refugees in Ramsey, Isle of Man. Jaleh managed a resettlement agency and Tom was an attorney who assisted with any legal problems.

CHAPTER ONE:
THE BROTHERS' NEXT MOVE

It was late afternoon in early February, 2014, when Dushan Sava and his American "stepbrother" Danilo Sandor returned to their hotel on the shore of Lake Bled, near Slovenia's capital, Ljubljana. The two young men had spent two days at the lake, taking advantage of the unseasonably warm weather to explore the lake on a couple of kayaks. They chose kayaks rather than hopping in one of the many "Dragon Boats" that just took you to the island and back. This way, they were able to explore the whole lake, not just the island.

Sitting in the hotel restaurant afterwards, they were still savoring their two days on the lake. "That was definitely the way to do it, Dani. I had no interest in sitting in a dragon boat with tourists, making small talk with them while listening to the oarsman rattle on with his spiel in broken English. That just didn't appeal to me."

"Exactly right, Dr. Dushansky. This way we got a little exercise, which God knows you could use. You still haven't lost all that weight you put on in prison. How long has it been since you sprung yourself—five, six months?"

Dushan ignored the comment. When Dani mentioned prison, Dushan revisited the brief twinge of unpleasantness he had felt the day before when he and Dani were in the lake boathouse investigating the various boating options. One of the boatmen helping some Italian people into a Dragon Boat had given Dushan the creeps. There was something about the man he didn't like, something unbalanced, evil even. That feeling reminded Dushan of one of the dreams he had as a little boy, a dream in which his mom was talking to him. She seemed to be saying she was a prisoner. The dream comforted him because he had been told by his stepparents that his mom was dead. The dream told him otherwise.

The feeling passed and the brothers decided on kayaks. They

spent that day and the next on the lake. Dushan let the memory of the boatman pass for now, took a drink of water, and responded to Dani's comment. "Well, the next time you see me, I'll be my former wiry self."

"Hah; you were never wiry, my brother. But I'll give you the benefit of the doubt. When you come visit me in Liverpool, we'll see how wiry you are."

Choosing to steer the conversation to something more interesting and less embarrassing than his weight, Dushan said, "So you've definitely decided on the University of Liverpool? That's a far cry from junior college in San Bernardino."

Dani grimaced at the memory of those days when the two stepbrothers ran away from Dani's abusive father with a desperate plan to live in San Bernardino and go to the junior college there. Now he smiled as his new plan of going to college in a new country filled his thoughts. "Yep. My Grandma Margaret told me she can help me get admitted through a 'legacy' admission. Apparently, one of her uncles was a wealthy alum who gave a fair sum of money to the University. Plus, she all but invited me to stay in the little cottage behind her house. I think I'd like that over a dorm."

Dushan put down his fork and said, "What about that bitch Carolyn? Did your grandma give you an update on what's going on with her? Remember when Lieutenant Ailshie said he was going to have the Liverpool cops pay Carolyn a visit?"

Dani chuckled and said, "Apparently he did just that. Margaret told me on the phone this morning that Carolyn was arrested and charged with your kidnapping. So far, she's enjoying the hospitality of a Liverpool jail. I guess Liverpool has jurisdiction in the case because the kidnapping took place there. There's gonna be some kind of pretrial hearing in June or July. You and your dad might have to go to that, and for sure to the trial, if there is one."

"You mean she might take a plea rather than risk a trial? Man, I sure hope she gets a clue and pleads guilty. I don't relish going all the way there and sticking around waiting to testify at her trial. I've got better things to do; getting my real identity back, for starters."

"I hear you, but even if there is a trial, at least you'll be around to see me enter the freshman class at the University."

"Sure, that would definitely be cool. But I've got a million things I've got to get settled here first. I need to get my birth certificate in

Belgrade. In fact, I **can't** do any more travelling on my 'stolen identity;' my first priority has to be to get that taken care of. I also need to enroll in some language courses, figure out the college situation. At some point I'll take a break and visit you in Liverpool."

Dani took a deep breath and looked Dushan in the eyes. "What kind of language courses? Slovenian? I got the impression from the conversations we had with your parents that they weren't too happy living in Ljubljana. The economy is in the toilet, your dad said his job might go away at any moment, your sisters said they weren't looking forward to going to high school in Ljubljana. Didn't you get the impression they were thinking of moving?"

"Yeah, it sure seemed that way. But I don't think they had a clear plan. Moving back to Belgrade didn't seem to be a viable alternative. The economy is even worse in Serbia than it is in Slovenia, and my mom especially doesn't feel comfortable with the idea of moving back there. That whole period of her life where she was a prisoner of Major Goran and the Serbian army left her with a deep-seated dread of ever going back there. My dad, too, doesn't relish the idea, even assuming he could get his old job back on the rivers."

"Well, if I may be so bold as to offer your family advice, why not consider a move to the Isle of Man? You remember what Angus said when we were there, before we headed over to Liverpool to meet my grandma? Lots of opportunities there. Your parents loved it there, and only moved back to Ljubljana to be closer to their families."

Dushan played with his food for a few moments before looking up at Dani. "I don't know how they would feel about that. But I'll definitely mention it to them."

Dani smiled, "I have a good feeling about this idea. Angus said there are some good schools in Douglas, even a university. Your sisters could enroll in one of the high schools there and you could enroll in the university."

Dushan chuckled as he finished the last bite of pasta. "I can see your self interest in all this. You'll be right across the Irish Sea from us, a few hours away instead of a few days away if I was living in Slovenia or Serbia."

Dani tried to put on a straight face. "I'm only trying to be practical. You know as well as I that nobody in your family is particularly happy living in Ljubljana."

"Well, you're right as far as my immediate family goes, but my

3

grandparents and aunts and uncles on both sides are pretty well situated and seem pretty content with their lives there. And my parents probably would want to stay close to them."

"Sure. And there's no reason your grandparents and aunts and uncles won't stay that way, even should your parents and the girls move away. It's a pretty short trip there by air, and plenty of vacation opportunities."

"Okay, okay, you've convinced me. I'll bring it up with them as soon as I have a chance when we get back. But first I'm gonna call Angus and talk over this idea with him. It would help to have some concrete options for my parents in terms of jobs." Dushan took a drink from his water glass and gave Dani a sly grin. "Now, you mentioned high schools in Douglas. How do you know anything about that? Have you been cooking up this plot on the sly?"

Dani tried not to smile. "It just so happens that Angus told me about a top-notch high school in Douglas called St. Ninians. And he said there are always job openings in the fishing and shipping industries, as well as in health care and social work. With your parents' years of experience, they'd have no trouble finding work. It's a great idea, my brother, you have to admit."

"I do admit it; like I said, I'll talk it up with them. You and I are going to do this together, as a matter of fact."

"Fine with me. If you do end up enrolling at the Isle of Man University, you and I can hook up during vacations. My winter break is a whole month, for God's sake! We could even invite my old Utah buddy Claude Prejean up for a week or so during winter break. He and I have been emailing each other a lot lately. He's now working in Trieste, Italy, and says he loves it; it's a whole lot more interesting than Utah was, and the job sounds pretty amazing."

Dushan pushed his plate away and raised his empty water glass to their waiter, who seemed to be studiously ignoring them. Putting the glass back down, Dushan asked Dani, "Did Claude say what he's doing exactly?"

"He's working with a university in Italy to preserve cliff limestone from various environmental and man-made threats. The region he's working in stretches from Trieste, Italy, to Dubrovnik, Croatia. It's contract work with the university, not a professorship, and he says the project is open-ended."

Dushan yawned and slowly rose to his feet. "We can figure out our plans later. For now we've got an awful lot on our plates. Tomorrow we should leave early for home, Ljubljana I mean. My mom texted me a little while ago and said some relatives had just arrived and they want to meet 'the brothers'."

"I have to say, Dushan, that you seem to be handling this reunion with your parents very, very well. How does it feel?"

Dushan didn't answer right away; the waiter had finally come over to fill his water glass. Dani asked for another caffe latte. As the waiter walked away, Dushan sat back down, turned back to Dani and said, "It may look like I'm taking it all in stride, but I'm not. This is going to take a fair amount of time, my brother. Mom and dad and I are going to have to get to know each other all over again. What am I saying! I hardly know them at all, especially my mom. I was snatched from her when I was six months old. With my dad, at least I spent four or five years with him, and I have a few nice memories of that time. And now I've got two teenage sisters to get to know. So, to answer your question—it feels good, yet strange at the same time. But there's a bond there, an attraction, love even. I just have to let this relationship grow and develop. I plan on spending every free moment with them. Rejoin the family. It may not be easy, but I'm pretty sure it will feel good."

CHAPTER TWO:
SHIMZA AND THE NEXT GENERATION

Marta was anxious the whole time the boys were gone. Lake Bled, two nights in a nice hotel, what was wrong with that? Clear weather for February, no danger of snow or sleet. Probably not a lot of people on the lake. She hadn't been to the lake in years, not since her camping trip in middle school. Still, when Dani and Dushan announced they would like to spend a couple of days on the lake, Marta felt a twinge of apprehension. Was she still remembering that stressful situation when her campmate almost died from eating a poisonous plant? Was she just being a worried mother? She told herself that was it, but she didn't fully believe it. She also felt a little hurt that Dushan would want to take off so soon for the lake. She wanted him all to herself; herself and Dimitri and the girls. She knew it would take a long, long time to get to know him, and she had wanted that time to continue uninterrupted from when the boys first arrived.

So she felt a mixture of joy and relief when she saw their rental car pull up in front of the house. She watched them through the kitchen window as they walked from the car to the house. They were smiling and talking like they had grown up together. But in fact, they **had** grown up together, or close to it. Marta had mixed feelings about that. On the one hand, Dushan was essentially stolen from her as a baby when she was kidnapped and forced to work in a Yugoslavian army camp. And then he was **actually** stolen from her husband Dimitri when Dimitri and Dushan were refugees in the Isle of Man back in 1999. But on the other hand, Dushan was then blessed with having Danilo as a stepbrother over in California for the next 14 years. That blessing helped mitigate the very poisonous family life he and Dani had to grow up in, poisoned by Dani's abusive father, Burt Sandor, the man who had arranged to steal Dushan from his real father, Marta's husband Dimitri, when Marta was still a prisoner of the Serbian Army.

But the fact that Dushan and Dani's closeness helped mitigate the mistreatment they experienced from Burt didn't change Marta's feelings of loss as a mother. *No doubt about it,* she thought, *I'm not letting him get away from me this time. Not until we've had him with us for a good long time!*

Marta's thoughts returned to the present as she walked to the front door to greet the young men. "Welcome home, guys! I've got a big surprise for you." Marta hugged them both as they came in. Dushan heard conversation in the living room, including two women's voices he didn't recognize. "Who are those ladies talking, mom?" he asked. Before Marta could answer, Dani grabbed Dushan's arm as if he was about to lead him down the entry hall into the living room.

Marta stopped them and said, "That's the surprise. Follow me." She walked in front and led them into the room. Dimitri and their two teenage daughters, Aisha and Shimza, were sipping tea and chatting with two older women. Everyone stood when Marta and the boys walked in. Marta did the introductions. "Boys, I'd like you to meet my grandma, Shimza Duritz, and Dimitri's aunt Adrijana Sava. I have always called my grandma "Nonna." Now that I have a daughter named Shimza, I think it'd probably be a good idea if we stick to Nonna."

Both Shimzas laughed, and the elder one, Nonna, said, "That was a title I chose for myself when Marta was a baby. Marta's mom, my half-Italian daughter-in-law, knew I wasn't fond of the Rom terms for grandma, Baba and Mamiya, so she suggested I be known by the Italian word, Nonna. It stuck. Just call me Nonna."

Marta put her hands on both boys' shoulders and said, "Nonna and Adrijana, these two fine young men are my son Dushan and his stepbrother Danilo."

Adrijana smiled and shook their hands. Addressing the assembled family members, she said, "I finally get to see the young man who was only a baby the last time I saw him. And his stepbrother! What an amazing story your mom has told us! But not all of it; I want to hear it all."

Nonna stepped forward and said, "I'm very, very pleased to meet you both. Everyone has been telling us parts of your remarkable story."

Dushan embraced her, more than a little misty-eyed. Dani shook her hand, and then embraced her as well. Smiling a little sheepishly, Dani said, "I feel like we're related, Nonna; more than related. When Dushan's mom and dad told us the story about you visiting them when she was barely pregnant, I felt a part of that story, too."

Nonna nodded and smiled. "I felt a similar recognition last night as Marta told me your story. It triggered something in me, the feeling I had experienced all those years ago when I visited Marta and Dimitri during their honeymoon. I knew Marta was pregnant then, something that not even Marta knew. At that time, I didn't know what to make of the feeling I had that a "disruption" in their baby's life would involve another family and another boy, so I just ignored the feeling."

Aisha spoke up and addressed Dushan and Dani. "Nonna was just starting to tell us about her work in Istanbul. Nonna, can you start over so they can hear it? And Adrijana, after that can you tell us how you, our mom and Amina found our dad in the Isle of Man?"

Adrijana smiled and said, "Certainly. I'm looking forward to hearing about your Nonna's exploits with the Rom people. Then I'll fill you in on our detective work; or rather, Lieutenant Angus Ailshie's detective work."

As Nonna motioned everyone to sit down, her expression fluctuated from a smile to a frown and back to a smile. "Maybe Dushan and Danilo don't know this, but all of us, except perhaps for you, Dani, have some gypsy blood in us. I prefer the term 'Rom,' as do most of our people. The terms 'Roma' and 'Romany' are also fine. The word 'gypsy' actually is a corruption of 'Egyptian.' In the old days Europeans thought the Rom people were Egyptian. We weren't, at least not originally. Our earliest ancestors left northern India and settled in Turkey and the Middle East in the middle ages. They began migrating to Europe in the 1400's."

Dimitri spoke up as Nonna took a sip from her iced tea. "My family lore holds that my great grandfather was a Rom elder of a group that travelled around Slovenia and Bosnia. Eventually, his family settled in Serbia. Some of them, like my grandfather, married non-Rom people, like my grandmother. My Aunt Adrijana here is their daughter, the sister of my mom, who's too ill and frail to be with us today."

Nonna resumed her story. "I'm one hundred percent Rom myself. I was born in Zagreb, Croatia, a state in the former Yugoslavia. My parents were Zoltan and Amalija Duritz." Putting on a serious face, Nonna said to the group, "Now write this down; you will be tested later." Everyone chuckled. Nonna resumed her story. "Our family had to flee to Trieste in 1921. I married a non-Rom man, Tomas Cecelja, in 1946 when I was 17. He was half Italian and half Slovenian. We had just moved to Ljubljana a year after World War II ended. Our son, Winston, named after Churchill, was born a year later. Winston married Elena Zupan, who was half Slovenian, half Serb, in 1964. Their daughter Marta, the mother of Dushan and the twins, was born in 1965. My husband Tomas died in 1977 when he was 66. Marta was about to begin 8th grade. Everyone got all that?"

Marta smiled as she motioned for her grandma to pause. "Nonna, I think the girls, and everyone else for that matter, would love to hear some of your adventures after Tomas died, especially what led you to move to Istanbul."

Dani smiled and interjected, "I would LOVE to hear it, Nonna. Just don't ask me to talk about MY family 'adventures'."

Dushan said, "You won't get away that easy, my brother. I'm sure everyone would love to hear the story that your grandma told us up in Liverpool a few weeks ago. Crooks, double agents, psychics—man, Cap'n Dante, your story is priceless!"

Laughter all around, and then Marta said, "Okay, it's gonna be family history time. First, let's let Adrijana give a little recap about how she and I found Dimitri living in Isle of Man as a refugee. Very interesting!"

Adrijana said, "Interesting, yes, but short. Really, it was due to Dimitri's friendship with the police officer in Ramsey, Isle of Man, Inspector Angus Ailshie. He found out that the refugee agencies in England had failed to keep their records up to date regarding Dimitri's placement, and got them to plug in all the current information. Then, in Ljubljana, when Marta, Amina and I happened to contact one of those agencies, we were told that Dimitri was settled in Ramsey. That did it; we dropped everything and took our first-ever airplane flight, to London, and took an Irish Sea ferry to Ramsey. After we found Dimitri, we were both overjoyed. And then when we learned that Dushan had been kidnapped, we were devastated. Eventually, Marta decided to remain in Ramsey with

Dimitri, and Amina and I returned home to Ljubljana. The twins were born in Ramsey, and after a couple of years, the family returned to Ljubljana as well."

Adrijana paused and looked over at Nonna Shimza. "But I want to hear Nonna's story. I've been hearing bits and pieces of it for years, but never the whole thing. Go ahead, my dear!"

Nonna took up the thread again. "Well, when my husband died, I decided to leave Ljubljana and move to Sofia, Bulgaria. This was the beginning of 1978. I thought that living in an ancient Rom community would help my vague ideas of helping my people take a more concrete shape.

"I was not quite 50 when I moved, had a master's degree and 15 years experience in social work. I also was a trained acupuncturist and herbalist and figured I could support myself in the short term by setting up an acupuncture clinic. Once I was on my feet financially, I looked for social work opportunities with the Rom community in Sofia, the Bulgarian capital. I was fortunate to attend a conference of Rom leaders from all across Europe seeking to address the problems of statelessness and lack of civil rights in the Rom community.

"After 15 years in Bulgaria, I learned of even greater opportunities working with the Rom of Turkey, who make up 14 percent of the population. In contrast to the discrimination they experienced throughout Eastern Europe, they enjoyed full civil rights in Turkish society, although they were not fully integrated and still experienced a certain amount of prejudice from potential landlords and employers.

"I attended another Europe-wide meeting of Rom leaders to address the problem of Rom statelessness and lack of civil rights. The group decided the best place to begin implementation of our plan would be Turkey.

"When I arrived in Istanbul, I spent at least a couple of months introducing myself to the many Rom groups and neighborhoods. Then an amazing thing happened. I met a somewhat well-off Rom family who'd managed to raise a daughter whose school success in a prestigious private high school earned her a full scholarship to an equally prestigious university."

At this point, the attentiveness of everyone, but especially the twins and the stepbrothers, became more focused. Aisha spoke up when Nonna took a sip of her tea. "Nonna, what was the name of the high school? One of our Turkish friends at school has a cousin who goes to a school called 'Robert' something. It doesn't sound very Turkish."

"'Robert College,' yes, that's it. It's actually a secondary school, grades 6 through 12, not a college as we think of the term. That's the amazing thing I'm talking about—this secondary school eventually led to another career for me: teaching 'Rom Studies' at Bosporus University in Istanbul. 'Robert College of Istanbul' is a private school in Istanbul but chartered in New York, in the United States. It's named after someone named Christopher Robert and has been in Istanbul for over 150 years. When I heard about the school and my new friends' daughter's success there, I had to check it out."

Aisha's twin sister Shimza joined the conversation. "Our Turkish schoolmate says she hopes to go to Bosporus University when she graduates. She says the schools are connected somehow, or used to be."

"Yes, they used to be connected. Robert College was the name of the university division and Robert Academy was the name of the secondary school. Some time in the 60's, I think, the Turkish government bought the university division and renamed it Bosporus University. Robert Academy became just Robert College. But still, the two continue to be very close, and many of the faculty members at BU are foreign, like most of the faculty at Robert College. It's safe to say that top graduates from Robert College have no trouble being admitted to Bosporus, not to mention universities in Europe and the States."

The twins looked at each other and then Shimza said to their mom, "This is amazing, Mom. Remember when I told you about our friend Suna's cousin who attends RC? I said it would be cool to attend Robert College. Suna says her cousin loves it, and loves the city of Istanbul, too."

Marta smiled and said, "Yes, I certainly got the message that you'd like to go there. But let's hear a little more about it from Nonna. Maybe it would be impossible for someone who's not a Turkish citizen to attend RC."

Nonna continued. "Well, that's correct. Robert College is required by law to only admit citizens of Turkey."

Dimitri asked, "What about children of Rom background? Even non-Turkish Rom kids are eligible?"

"If they're citizens, yes, indeed they are, as are the Greek,

Armenian, Kurdish and Jewish citizens of Turkey. I told you how I'd been teaching one course every term at BU called "'Sociology of the Rom People.'" I was hired to teach that course through my acquaintance with the one of the academic deans."

Dimitri asked, "So, you've been teaching there how long?"

"This is my twelfth year. But it will be my last. Although I've loved my teaching career there, teaching isn't what I set out to do, and I'm going to see if I can get back into social work among the Rom people. But not in Turkey."

Marta said, "Nonna, are you giving up on Turkey? I thought you loved it there."

"I did love it there. But things have changed. The government, for one thing. It's becoming more and more repressive. Scary, actually. I don't know where things are headed. But I guess I don't have the energy to continue dealing with the situation. It's time for a change. I've heard of a fairly new social program in Liverpool that's devoted entirely to assisting the newly arrived Rom communities there. Mostly from Eastern Europe, where I spent the bulk of my career. So, we'll see. I'll be moving to Liverpool in June to check out the situation."

Dushan gave Dani a furtive glance and then looked at his mother and father to see what their reactions were to this latest surprise from Nonna. Dani nodded his head almost imperceptibly. Dushan then said to Marta, "Mom, I didn't get a chance to mention this to you, but Dani and I were chatting with Angus about the Isle of Man when we were at Dani's grandma's house in Liverpool. He happened to mention that the Isle of Man job market is pretty good right now, across the board. Seems companies and agencies are having trouble keeping employees; they keep leaving for greener pastures in the UK proper."

Dimitri leaned back in his chair and said, "That's interesting. Did he say anything about schools there? When we lived there back in the early 2000's, we hadn't paid much attention to the school situation, although your mom and I had talked about getting your sisters in daycare."

Dani spoke up. "As a matter of fact, Angus told us that if we ever wanted to go to college there, the Isle of Man University was pretty good. I told him I was already planning on attending Liverpool U. But Dushan looked interested."

Marta chuckled and asked, "You two didn't happen to look into high schools there, did you? Just out of curiousity?"

Dani blushed and said, "I admit, I did do a bit of sleuthing. There's a really top-notch high school in Douglas called St. Ninians."

Shimza and Aisha perked up. Aisha looked at her dad and said, "We should go take a look at the school. Our spring break is in three weeks. What do you say?"

Dimitri stood, stretched and said, "We'll see. Let's talk about that later. But for now, I'm not going to let these boys get off without them telling Nonna a little about their adventures, and letting us all know what plans they have in mind." He retrieved a platter of dolma from the dining table, set it on the coffee table and returned to his seat.

Dushan spoke first, "Wow, after hearing about Isle of Man, and the possibility of my family moving there, the idea occurs to me to check out the Isle of Man University for myself. But before I do that, I need to take care of the small matter of my official identity. I travelled here on a false identity, not a stolen identity as my esteemed but deeply confused brother Danilo asserts."

Dani presented the group with a mock-serious expression of puzzlement. Then, with a wink at the twins and just a hint of a smile, said to Dushan, "What do you mean? You're the one who's confused. Did you or did you not appropriate the identity of a young man named Douglas Armitage?"

Marta's laughter preceded the rest of the group's chuckles. Turning to Nonna, she said, "Dushan's story is almost too good to be true. I hardly know which part of it is stranger—being stolen as a child; being imprisoned as a teenager for a murder that never happened; escaping unscathed from a fatal auto accident while being transported to an immigration prison where he would be deported to his 'home' in England; adopting the identity and travel documents of the unfortunate young man killed in the accident; or going to college in New York using that young man's identity."

Dushan smiled mock-triumphantly and said to his brother, "You're just jealous, Cap'n Dante. And maybe a little embarrassed at having had to spend a Utah winter in a snowbound mountain cabin with a Frenchman named Claude."

Laughing, the twins spoke up almost at the same time with the same demand, "Stop it. We want it all, the whole story. We'll be the judges of whose story is more believable, or at least more entertaining!"

For the next hour, with Dushan and Dani reeling off their stories and interrupting one another as they did so, the evening passed from early to late. Shimza The Younger, as she decided to start calling herself, at least as long as Nonna was present, spoke up after Dani had paused to take a drink, "Dani, if you really are going to go to college in Liverpool, I think we—the whole family—should think about your idea of us moving to the Isle of Man. What's Liverpool like?"

"I'm hardly in a position to know much about Liverpool. I was only born there; we moved to California when I was a toddler. But basically, the deal is this. My Greek-English grandma offered to let me live in her little cottage rent free, and says she can probably help in making sure Liverpool University will admit me."

Dushan jumped in, "You're assuming, and it's a BIG assumption, ladies and gentlemen, that your grades are good enough. By the way, refresh my memory, what was your GPA in high school?"

Dani shrugged and smiled, "You're just jealous that I was so much more well-rounded than you, the big nerd-brain on campus."

"Interesting that you use the term 'well rounded' to refer to your attitude about high school," Dushan said, laughing. Everyone chuckled, but seemed to be waiting for Dani to spell out exactly how well rounded he was.

Eyebrows raised and a mildly triumphant expression on his face, Dani said, "You may recall, dear brother of mine, that it was I who managed to board the moving freight train in Southern California. And after being thrown off unceremoniously by a couple of scoundrels, I spent almost half a year in a ski cabin in the Utah mountains, not only surviving but caring for a seriously injured skier for much of that time. And then I managed to return to our home, which was when I discovered my talent for advanced sleuthing, my dear Dushansky. There I discovered that our abusive dad, Burt Sandor that is, had killed himself after killing a federal agent who had discovered that Burt **bought** you from Carolyn. What's more, everyone told me you were convicted of my murder and then killed in an auto accident. I knew that you were still alive—I saw you in my mind's eye, speaking to me—and I tracked you down. Do I need to remind you that it was I who cleared you of the murder charge, and refused to believe it was you who was killed in that horrible auto accident in Arizona?"

With an equally impressive mock-serious expression on his face, Dushan replied, "I think you're trying to suggest your skill at overcoming diversity was unmatched. But you have only to recall that I was a guest of the California Department of Corrections for a spell, for a murder that never happened. Having no official, legitimate, identity, I chanced upon an opportunity to acquire yet another false identity, one which would allow me to embark on a more normal life as a student; and then who knows how long I could keep that identity? My first false identity, as a Sandor, lasted for about 15 years before being traded in for this new false identity as Douglas Armitage, the unfortunate young man killed in the automobile accident in the Arizona desert as I was being transported to the deportation prison near the Mexican border."

Nonna's smile was huge and her eyes sparkled. "As if those stories weren't amazing enough, now we get to the part that brought us all together, the part where these two remarkable young men not only found each other but found us. Marta and Dimitri told us how you showed up here, presenting yourselves as tourist friends of that English detective Angus Ailshie. I, for one, would love to hear more about how you ran into him and how he finally tracked down Dushan's kidnapper, that Carolyn monster."

Dani batted Dushan's hand away from the Dolma platter and said with a mock-stern smile, "It's my turn, Dr. Dushansky, to regale these folks with yet another amazing tale of clever detective work." But before Dani could continue, Dushan jumped in, "Pure luck, you mean. Please continue, and try not to exaggerate too much."

Sitting back in his chair and smiling at Nonna and the others, Dani said, "Well, there was a little bit of sleuthing on my part. When my esteemed brother here first came to live with us in California, he was not quite five and a year younger than me. He used to tell us stories of things he and Dimitri did back in the Isle of Man, their social activities and friends." Turning back to Dushan, Dani said, "For some reason, your description of a place you called the 'Baha'i Centre' stuck in my mind. Probably because you said you and Dimitri used to go to parties there, and you talked about that place like it was your second home. As we grew up, you would always talk about those days and swore you would go back there and find your real dad. So when we were aimlessly traipsing around the island, the thought occurred to me to ask someone where the Baha'i Centre was—and we managed to almost literally run into Jaleh Kilpatrick."

Marta said, "When my friends and I found Dimitri on the Isle of Man, he introduced us to Jaleh and her husband Thomas. During the time we lived there we became friends with Tom and Jaleh and got to know a little about their religion."

Nonna eagerly jumped in, "I'm familiar with that religion. The Rom family I told you about, the one whose daughter was a standout student at Robert College and Bosphorus University, were followers of that religion." Pausing for a few seconds with a thoughtful look on her face, she said to Marta, "If you and the family did decide to relocate to the Isle of Man, I'd bet Jaleh and Thomas could help you with the transition. And I would love to 'hook up,' as you kids say, with the Kilpatricks."

Dani said, "I think I'll contact them when I get back to Liverpool next week, maybe even pay them a visit on the Isle itself if I have time. I'll let them know what's on everyone's mind."

The twins spoke up practically at the same time, "We're Facebook friends of theirs. We can keep them informed of our plans. This should be exciting!"

"Not too exciting to keep me from going to bed," Dimitri said with a yawn. "It's almost 1 a.m."

The yawn was catching, and gradually the family members straggled off to bed.

CHAPTER THREE:
DUSHAN GETS LEGAL

For the next week after the boys' return from their mini-vacation at Lake Bled, they wanted nothing more than to spend as much time as possible getting to know Dushan's family. Adrijana and Nonna left to return to their jobs the morning after their reunion with everyone, so Dushan and Dani had Marta, Dimitri and the girls to themselves. During the daytime, they alternated between accompanying Marta to her job with the city and visiting Dimitri at his job on the river. Even the girls had plans for them—they talked their school's English department head into inviting the boys to give a talk on their experiences. Aisha and Shimza were bursting with pride.

Because of the sudden reappearance of winter later that week, offices and schools were closed and the river was too icy for Dimitri's fishing operations to continue. The family spent almost the entire time indoors, which made for a very cozy getting-to-know-you experience. Marta and Dimitri filled the boys in on what those years had been like after Dushan's abduction and Dimitri's lonely years on the Isle of Man. The girls told them all about school life in Ljubljana. But the most wrenching subject of conversation was Dushan's abduction and upbringing in California. No one had a dry eye during those conversations. The girls were particularly intrigued by Dushan's accounts of seeing and hearing his parents talking to him in his dreams. They, as well as Marta and Dimitri, were also amazed by how often Dushan and Dani communicated each other in dreams and times of stress, like when Dushan survived the crash of the vehicle transporting him to the immigration prison in Arizona, or earlier when Dushan had a "vision" of Dani living in a cabin in the wilderness after their separation.

In mid-March, Dani left to do a little touring before he had to return to Liverpool. With the weather still too iffy for Dimitri to return to work on the river, he and Dushan paid a visit to Aunt Adrijana in Belgrade, a few weeks after she had returned home from the family reunion in Ljubljana. Once there, they learned that in order to obtain a Serbian birth certificate and passport, Dushan would be required to pass a rudimentary test in the Serbian language. Even though Dushan's long dormant ability to speak Serbian was slowly awakening with Dimitri's tutoring, Dushan decided to take a crash course in the language. Adrijana offered to let him stay with her while he enrolled in a three-week intensive language course she had found for him. He would take care of his citizenship paperwork as soon as he completed the course.

Adrijana was overjoyed at being able to play host, and immediately showed Dushan the spare room in her home that would be his during the time it took for him to complete the language course and obtain his citizenship documents. Dimitri had to get back to work, and returned to Ljubljana soon after Dushan got settled in. At the end of the course he would return to help Dushan with his citizenship application. After that, he would take Dushan back to Ljubljana.

For the next three weeks, Dushan did little else but go to class and study. During his only day off each week, he and his great aunt took in the sights of Belgrade. At his request, Adrijana showed him the Kalemegdan Fortress, Belgrade's oldest tourist attraction, dating back to 3 B.C. Marta had told him and Dani the story of how Milan took her there on her first tour of Belgrade after their all-night escape from Sarajevo, and it was first on the list of things Dushan wanted to see. After an hour touring that impressive structure, Adrijana showed Dushan the building where she used to own a little restaurant, and the café where Dushan's parents first met across the river.

After Dushan completed the grueling course in the Serbian language (which he called "a fair jaw-cracker" of a language, quoting Sam Gamgee from Lord of the Rings), Dimitri returned to Belgrade to help Dushan navigate the city's nationality bureau and obtain Dushan's birth certificate and passport.

"Now, I'm official—Dushan Danilo Sava," Dushan announced.

Adrijana gave him a puzzled look and said, "Wait, wait. You never had a middle name as far as I know, and Danilo is your step-brother's name."

"I now have a middle name. It was simple. Once I had my birth certificate, I applied for my passport and put Danilo in the blank for middle name. Much to dad's relief, the clerk never even checked."

Dimitri chuckled. Adrijana raised an eyebrow, half amazed and half amused, and said, "Are you sure you didn't use a little of that 'push' your mom used to talk about?"

Dushan laughed. "Maybe just a little. But really, auntie, I don't think those clerks look twice at the forms. I could have put 'Clinton' in the blank. Well, maybe not Clinton."

Adrijana was about to point out how risky it would have been to mention the name Clinton to a Serb in Belgrade, but decided not to revisit that horrible time. "Your dad tells me the family has decided to move to Douglas and enroll the girls in that private school. And you'll be applying to the university there. I think that's wonderful, even though you guys will be a lot farther from Belgrade."

Dushan said, "We all thought it would be a great idea. Mom has a pretty good chance of getting a job at the general hospital there, and it looks like dad will have a job at the port. I won't be that far from Liverpool, so Dani and I can stay close."

Adrijana smiled. "Speaking of Danilo, have you heard from him since he left your parents' home in Ljubljana? I very much enjoyed talking with him when I visited you all."

"I talked to him a couple of times since then. In September he'll be starting his freshman year at the University of Liverpool. No major in mind yet, although he said he'll take the prerequisites for some kind of geology or civil engineering major. He developed a spark of curiosity during the months he worked for that Canadian guy's mining company in Utah. You remember him talking about Claude?"

"Yes, I certainly do. Your stepbrother is one very fortunate young man to have run into Mr. Prejean, even though I'm quite sure Prejean feels equally fortunate to have run into Dani."

"Well, Dani's on his way to visit Claude right now, in Trieste. Claude's working on some kind of geological survey for an Italian university. I got to talk to Claude on Skype a week ago but Dani hadn't arrived yet. I told him Dani is probably taking his sweet time getting there. He must be touring around Italy a bit. It sounds like they've turned out to be good friends. I can't wait to meet Claude myself when I get a chance. For the time being, I've got a few things I need to get done when I go home, like fill out my college application."

In early May, Dushan and his father took the train back home to Ljubljana. With his Serbian birth certificate showing his birth in Belgrade to a Slovenian mother, he was now ready to obtain his Slovenian citizenship, which he couldn't do before as a stateless nonentity without a recognized identity. Dushan had a vague dream to become a dual-national human rights activist who grew up in the UK and the USA and spoke three languages. Somewhere lurking in his mind as an unformed thought cloud was the idea of working in some kind of international agency.

CHAPTER FOUR:
A DANGEROUS DEAL

Carolyn Markos still couldn't quite believe that the authorities had agreed to release her on bail; *in a kidnapping case, no less!* She knew her release never would have happened had it not been for her second cousin Burt's mother, Margaret Sandor, who had not only paid her bail bond, but had convinced the authorities to order her 52-year-old niece Carolyn to live in Margaret's home pending trial. Margaret's persuasive skill was legendary in the Greek-English-Hungarian clan of which she was an honored matriarch. She was also a genuine elder of the community, about to celebrate her 88th birthday on June 12, 2014. She had given birth to Burt when she was 46 years old, somewhat to the embarrassment of her even older husband.

Despite Carolyn's gratitude to Margaret for springing her from jail, she was more than a little out of sorts. *I've got to wear this bloody electronic bracelet monitor 24/7. And I can't even take a walk outside the property without the cursed thing alerting the police!* Carolyn had been arrested in December of last year and spent the next five months in jail before her release on bail.

The pretrial hearing was eight weeks away and the first of several plea-bargaining sessions with the prosecuting attorney was in two weeks. She had little hope the government would agree to anything less than a prison term. Her lawyer told her a conviction for kidnapping could result in a prison sentence of anywhere from two to twenty years, and that a grant of probation was extremely unlikely. Carolyn found her lawyer's statement to be very depressing, and at the same time annoying. She could tell that he wasn't interested in working hard on getting her the best deal possible.

In the meantime, Carolyn's spirits were raised when Margaret handed her the telephone and whispered, "My cousin, Charlotte

Bekas, is on the line." Carolyn had written to Charlotte soon after Carolyn's release on bail for the kidnapping of four-year-old Dushan Sava in 1999. Carolyn flinched every time she was reminded of her crime. After having posed as Dushan's babysitter, Carolyn handed him over to her cousin Burt Sandor and the three of them fled to California, where Dushan lived the next 14 years or so as Dushan Sandor, stepbrother of Danilo Sandor. When Burt's abusive personality finally pushed the then-teenage brothers too far, they attacked him, stole his car, and took off.

Carolyn had lived with Burt and Irene and the boys only during the few years they lived in San Francisco. After the family moved to southern California, Carolyn stayed in San Francisco until a startling event made her decide to leave the United States. She would have lived in San Francisco happily ever after had it not been for a chance encounter with her ex-husband, Trevor Owens.

Trevor and his new bride were on their honeymoon trip from their home in Australia to California and then to the British Isles. They were just finishing their California visit and were headed for the Isle of Man, a "crown protectorate" of Britain in the Irish Sea. Trevor and Carolyn had lived there before their divorce, and Trevor was eager to introduce his new wife to all his friends there. Carolyn worried that Trevor would probably tell his friends of his encounter with Carolyn in San Francisco. If the police back home got wind of her whereabouts, she could be extradited. In a panic, she left for Canada on the next leg of her flight from justice, and eventually she made her way back home to England.

Inevitably, Carolyn's past caught up with her after fleeing Canada for the UK. She hoped to live in Liverpool under the radar, but someone in her family's circle of acquaintances must have seen her and told someone. After that, it was only a matter of time before Margaret learned of Carolyn's return. When Lieutenant Ailshie brought Dani and Dushan over to meet Margaret, she learned of the details of Carolyn's crime and alerted the authorities of her whereabouts.

Carolyn was deeply ashamed of what she had done, and while in the Liverpool jail she vowed to write a lengthy letter of confession to her second cousin Charlotte if she ever got out of jail. Charlotte was shocked and troubled by what she read. After all her many visits to the Sandor family in southern California, to learn that little Dushan was not a bona fide adopted son, but rather a **stolen** child, just made Charlotte sick.

Charlotte stopped visiting the Sandors after her husband, Greg Bekas, also a distant relative of the Sandor clan, found Burt Sandor repulsive and refused to accompany Charlotte on her visits to Irene and the boys. Soon after Burt's wife Irene died, Greg cashed out his partnership shares in his Los Angeles shipping company and invested some of the money in a small start-up freight-forwarding company in Perth Amboy, New Jersey. As Charlotte had done during their time in Los Angeles, she worked as the company office manager.

Their move to Jersey took place when the boys were still young and living in San Francisco, as was Carolyn. Charlotte only heard from her sporadically. After sending Charlotte a few letters from San Francisco, Carolyn started sending the occasional postcard from Canada—no return address—and even those eventually stopped.

Because Perth Amboy was only about an hour from Princeton University, Charlotte seized the opportunity to apply to the Master's program in Creative Writing there. She was 60 years old when she applied for admission, and worried that her age would count against her. But it didn't, probably because of the quality of the writing samples she submitted with her application. Throughout the two-year program, her professors were very impressed with her writing, in particular a short story she wrote in her final semester.

The story was closely based on an incident in the life of her husband Greg's nephew, Makelle Ringhiera. Charlotte named the main character in her story "Miguel Barandilla" and based Miguel's fictional life on her husband's nephew's life. Makelle was the son of Greg's younger sister, Melina Bekas, and her Italian-Eritrean husband, Takeste Ringhiera. Melina, a UK citizen, and Takeste, a dual Eritrean and Italian citizen, immigrated to the US in 1964 from Liverpool with their three-year-old son "Makelle," named after Takeste's mother's hometown in Ethiopia's Tigre Province. Melina, Takeste and Makelle settled in a small working-class city on the Sacramento delta in northern California, where Takeste worked for Dow Chemical and Melina taught at the local junior high school.

In Charlotte's fictional story, set in 1979 like the real-life story, her fictional character Miguel had just graduated from high school and was about to set off for college. Like Makelle, Miguel grew up in that same small town on the delta. Miguel was the son of an immigrant father from Spain who had served in the US Army in World War II, and a homegrown Okie woman who was proud of having a "Heinz 57 Varieties" ethnic background—Irish, English, Native American and African American. She grew up on a farm, became a teacher and taught school in every town they moved to as the Army transferred her husband around the country throughout his 30-year Army career. Their last move was to the little town on the delta, Miguel's hometown.

Miguel's parents made damn sure he toed the line, buckled down and got good grades in school. Miguel didn't rebel very much against their rules because he was motivated by the strong desire to get into a good college, far enough away, so he wouldn't have to live at home.

Charlotte portrayed Miguel as not very self-aware in high school, even though he tended to be inquisitive, smart and hedonistic. He applied to and was accepted into the University of California, Santa Barbara, a college both academically excellent and very much a party school. Miguel was particularly excited by the fact that the school was 350 miles away; much preferable to San Jose State, which was only 50 miles from his home and arguably—at least in his parents' opinion—within commuting range.

In the story, Charlotte described Miguel's sex life in high school as somewhat disappointing—he had enough sex, but a poor attitude about it. He carried that attitude toward girls into UCSB and immediately got into a sexual relationship with Judy, a co-ed in "Frosh Camp," the university's attempt at freshman orientation.

Charlotte glossed over how much or how good their sex was, or the quality of their relationship, and got right to the point—Miguel got his part-German, part-Gypsy, girlfriend pregnant. Miguel at first denied responsibility for it—accusing Judy of having sex with her old boyfriend back home in La Jolla during Thanksgiving break, when Miguel was visiting his folks at home. But then Miguel accepted responsibility and agreed to help pay for Judy's abortion. Miguel had no memory of ever seeing Judy after that.

That was the lion's share of Charlotte's story—that highly emotional and stressful month in Santa Barbara in December 1979. There was constant arguing between Miguel, Judy and their friends, on top of the stress of finding an abortion doctor (whom she found in Los Angeles). The story also showed how Miguel dealt with his guilt afterwards—he decided on a career as a public interest lawyer fighting sex trafficking in the San Francisco Bay Area.

Charlotte was very pleased with her story, and so were her professors, especially the chairwoman of the department, who happened to be on Charlotte's thesis committee. Professor Ola Lawson loved the story so much she urged Charlotte to submit it to the "NYC Midnight" creative writing competition. Charlotte did and, to her great surprise, she won. Not only won, but won a few hundred dollars and publication in Great American Short Stories.

The prize hardly made a difference in her material life, as the income from their freight-forwarding company was more than adequate for their lifestyle. It made even less of a difference to her personal life when, a month after Charlotte received notice of her story's upcoming publication, Greg passed away from a sudden aneurism in his chest. Suddenly Charlotte found herself "unmoored," a term Greg used to love to say. The grief, shock and disbelief gradually subsided, and Charlotte became less entangled with the company after she hired a manager to run things.

The story's publication had a very beneficial effect on one member of the family—Makelle Ringhiera, Greg's nephew. Like Miguel in the story, Makelle had also gotten his girlfriend, Heike, pregnant. When she announced her intention to get an abortion, Makelle suffered from guilt his whole life and never saw her again after she left for Los Angeles to get the abortion. Seeing Miguel's published story out there had a healing effect on him. Charlotte's story gave him hope; it let him see how Miguel processed his guilt and moved on in his life, especially Miguel's career as a public interest lawyer.

Makelle and Charlotte always managed to keep in touch throughout his youth and young adulthood. Even though Charlotte was technically some sort of "aunt-in-law," she was only 10 years older than Makelle. He visited her many times over the years, even after becoming a lawyer specializing in international criminal law. Early in his career with a San Francisco law firm Makelle mostly did international business transactions. Soon, however, Makelle became more interested in international criminal law and started taking a few of those cases on a "pro bono" basis. After working on a dozen or so of those, he tried his hand at teaching a course at Golden Gate University in San Francisco one night a week for a couple of semesters. That was when he discovered he enjoyed teaching law, and soon quit the law firm and moved over to the academic side full time.

Makelle arrived for his latest visit to Charlotte almost a week ago, in mid-May, ten days after finishing a nine-month visiting professorship at Liverpool University. He was 53 years old and in the prime of his very successful legal career. He was footloose at that time, having leased his San Francisco house to tenants for a year. The lease would not end for another three months, although his renters had told him in no uncertain terms they would love to stay in the house on a month-to-month basis should he decide to prolong his stay in Europe. He therefore decided to keep that option open, and in the meantime accepted an invitation to participate in a weeklong panel that summer at Princeton Law School on international criminal law—something to do with national jurisdictional disputes over related crimes occurring in two countries. Before returning to the US, he had spent the first week after his visiting professorship ended visiting the Isle of Man, in the Irish Sea across from Liverpool.

Makelle was now staying with Charlotte in Perth Amboy and commuting to Princeton daily to participate in the panel. One evening he dropped a little bomb on her. "You'll never guess who I ran into at Liverpool University just before the end of the term. Actually, I didn't run into her; she looked me up and attended my last lecture. We had dinner after that."

"Who? Someone I know?"

"You only knew Heike as the girl I got pregnant in 1979. You put her in your story as Miguel's girlfriend, Judy, who had an abortion and dropped out of Miguel's life forever."

"What? You mean Heike looked you up after all those years? Why? Did she want to kill you, or blackmail the successful international lawyer to get more money?"

"Neither. It turns out there never was an abortion. She had the baby! All these years I thought she had gone to LA, had the abortion and disappeared. The baby was born in August of 1980, a girl Heike named Jaelle."

"Wow—and you had no idea? She must have disappeared from your life completely."

"That's exactly right, just like Judy in your story. I never saw Heike again. Of course, at the time that was okay with me. I never forgot Heike, though, or my guilt over getting her pregnant and the whole abortion trauma."

Makelle got up, stretched and walked over to his aunt's piano. As he plunked out a few notes of "Summertime," Charlotte came up behind him and massaged his neck and shoulders. "You're all tense. This must have been a rough time for you."

"Well, actually, when Heike came up to me in Liverpool after my last public presentation on the refugee crisis in Europe, her first words to me set me free. It was amazing. I recognized her immediately, but before I could tense up, she gave me a big smile. I started to tear up and hugged her. For some reason, the relief I felt was completely free of any guilt. I must have given her a puzzled look, because her first words to me were, 'It never happened, Makelle, there was no abortion. I had the baby. She's a beautiful, talented young woman. She takes after her papa.'"

Charlotte sat down on the piano bench next to Makelle and played a little of the left hand part of Summertime. Makelle, misty-eyed, turned to her and said, "You know, Charlotte, that day turned out to be one of the best days—maybe **the** best day—of my life. Heike and I had dinner that evening. She told me her whole life story and I told her mine. She said she had never married, and I told her I had never married. She raised Jaelle all by herself in Heike's parents' home in Cologne, Germany. Jaelle grew up all over the map and now lives in Liverpool. She's a musician, plays bouzouki and sings in what she calls her 'gypsy band.' Apparently, she gets gigs all over the city."

Charlotte said, "Wait, wait, wait. This sounds too good to be true. How could Heike have just run into you accidentally?"

"It wasn't really an accident. Heike had come over to visit her daughter for a few weeks and saw a flyer advertising my talk on the refugee crisis on a table in one of the university-district cafes. The rest is history. Oh, and get this—Heike gave Jaelle my last name, Ringhiera! I guess it was common in those days to give the baby the father's surname"

Makelle stood and walked over to the fireplace mantle. Picking up a framed portrait, he said, "I love this photo of my mom and dad. Did Uncle Greg take it? Where was this?"

"Yeah, Gregory was an avid photographer. The photo was taken before my time with Gregory. Don't forget, he was 15 years older than me. This was when he visited your dad's parents in Eritrea, down on the Red Sea coast at their brewery in Massawa. Your parents had both just graduated from Asmara University, in Eritrea's capital up in the highlands. Your mom's degree was in Anthropology and your dad's was in Chemistry. They were headed to Liverpool. Your mom's and Gregory's family offered to put them up during Melina's pregnancy with you, while Takeste did his master's in chemical engineering."

"So, this must have been, what, early 60's?"

"Right. 1960. June, if memory serves. They were lucky to leave when they did. Six months later some military officers attempted a coup in Ethiopia, including Eritrea, which was still a province back then. The leaders of the coup attempt had planned to implement a nationalist agenda all over the country to take over the larger businesses. Your granddad's brewery was a potential takeover target, of course, with him being Italian and the company being the largest beer monopoly in the country. Luckily, his being married to an Eritrean woman saved him. He had some years earlier transferred ownership of the company to his wife's brother, thereby keeping it in the family and safe from expropriation. In any event, the coup never got very far, and the monarchy remained in power."

Makelle set down the framed picture and said, "I knew most of that story, but never quite got why my mom—a Greek UK citizen—ended up in East Africa."

Charlotte smiled and said, "Gregory always called her his African sister. She had heard that there were lots of Greeks in Ethiopia and decided to take a break from her junior year at L.U. and tour Ethiopia. She loved Asmara so much she transferred to Asmara University to finish her B.A. in anthropology. That's where she met your father, and they were instantly smitten with each other. I'm guessing your dad's striking African-Italian looks had something to do with that, those blue eyes, olive skin, and nappy African hair that he wore in the 'dreadlocks' style. You're definitely more of a Ringhiera than a Bekas in the looks department, except that you don't do your hair in dreadlocks."

Charlotte's mention of Asmara reminded Makelle of his so-far-unfulfilled desire to go there someday. "Mom used to tell me what a great city Asmara was. She hated Massawa, though—'too damn hot... all the time!'—was her mantra when dad spoke fondly of his dad's second home at the brewery."

Charlotte laughed and said, "Gregory always said it was Liverpool and the Bekas clan that saved his little sister from 'going native.'"

Charlotte could tell that her nephew was getting tired and would be wanting to go to bed soon, so she decided to bring up an urgent, but very embarrassing, topic—her cousin Carolyn's predicament. "I received a very disturbing letter today, Makelle. It's from Carolyn Markos, an old friend from Liverpool, a distant cousin, in fact. She tells me she's been in jail for something serious."

Makelle's expression changed instantly from distracted and sleepy to interested and wide-awake. He walked back to the couch and sat down. "So, tell me more. Is she the one Uncle Greg talked about, the one who lived in San Francisco with Irene and Burt and the boys for a while?"

"That's her. I used to visit them every couple of months; I loved San Francisco and so did Carolyn and Irene. Plus, the three of us basically grew up together in Liverpool. I was like an older sister to Carolyn since she was an only child. Our families were related and maintained the connection. Gregory hardly ever went with me; he said he couldn't stand Burt. I kept up the visits even after the family moved to Victorville without Carolyn, which was a few years after Burt and Irene's second son Markos died. But when Irene died, especially after Carolyn left San Francisco without telling anyone, I stopped visiting the family. I really loved the two stepbrothers, Dani and Dushan, but couldn't stand Burt. And neither could the boys, it seemed to me."

"Where did Carolyn go? You said she's in jail in Liverpool. How did she end up back there?"

"I had no idea until a little while ago. Like I said, I didn't even know she had left San Francisco. But then I received a couple of postcards from her. They were postmarked in Canada but had no return address. And all she said was stuff like 'I'm okay. I miss you.' No mention of where she was or what she was doing. And now this letter."

Charlotte got up, walked over to the roll-top desk and retrieved the letter. "Here, read it and tell me what you think."

Makelle examined the envelope, noticing the UK postage stamps and the Liverpool return address. "The return address is a preprinted 'Margaret Sandor' sticker from Amnesty International. I recognize her name. Isn't she Burt's mother? I thought you said Carolyn was in jail."

"She had been released on bail just before she wrote this letter.

Read it and we can talk about what to do."

Makelle took out the page from the envelope. The handwriting was shaky and hard to read. "Sheesh, this is worse than a doctor's handwriting. I'll read it out loud and you can help me if I can't make something out. Here goes.

"Dear Charlotte,

I hope you're sitting down when you read this; it's pretty awful news. I just got out of jail in Liverpool. I did something absolutely terrible back in 1999 and now I'm paying for it. I kidnapped a four-year-old boy, pretending to be his babysitter, and took him to California to be raised as my cousin Burt's son. The boy, Dushan, grew up there thinking his real parents were dead.

But I want to explain how it happened. I really, truly, don't think I was in my right mind when I did it. In fact, I believe I was coerced—by Burt, and by a Bosnian gangster guy who talked me into doing some illegal adoptions. Well, I got caught doing the illegal adoptions, had my bank account frozen, and I owed the gangster LOTS of money. He was threatening to kill me if I didn't pay him. Just at that point, Burt calls me asking me to adopt a kid for him, a kid who would "replace" his own dying little son. Burt offered me a TON of money to do it for him. Charlotte, I can't really express how powerful this combination of factors was, or how it overrode my own sense of morality. I was absolutely terrified of that gangster, and Burt convinced me (you KNOW how persuasive he could be!) that I should "adopt" one of those refugee kids from the Balkans who were flooding the British Isles in those awful days.

Charlotte, I did it! I did the deed. But I need you to hear me out, in my own voice, and talk to me. Please, can I call you? I'm living with Burt's mother, Margaret, and she gave me your address and phone number. I'll call you in a week. My kidnapping case is on hold for the time being, but soon I'll have to go to trial or do some kind of plea bargain."

Makelle put down the letter on the end table and looked over at Charlotte, who was watching him for some sort of reaction. "I don't know what to say, auntie. This is awful. Kidnapping! It makes me sick to think of that poor boy, not to mention his parents. Did she call you yet?"

"Yes, a couple of days before you got here from Liverpool. We talked for almost an hour and she poured her heart out to me. Makelle, it was so sad; a sad and awful story! And such a strange one! You know, after I spoke with Carolyn, I called Margaret later the same day and got her take on the situation. She filled me in on some of the more amazing parts of the story. I could hardly believe it, but

Dushan—the one who was kidnapped—showed up on Margaret's front porch last December, with his so-called 'stepbrother' in tow. The two boys, Dushan and Danilo, are 19 and 20 years old, respectively. They were accompanied by a retired police inspector from the Isle of Man, where the kidnapping had begun."

Makelle rubbed his eyes and let his breath out slowly. "So, what does Carolyn want you to do, besides offer your shoulder to cry on? Does she have an attorney?"

"Yes, she says she has a court-appointed lawyer, but she complains that the lawyer is urging her to "plead to the sheet," meaning just admit everything and let the judge sentence her to whatever term he thinks appropriate. Carolyn, understandably, wants to do better than that. She thinks she might have some kind of viable "coercion defense," based on her fear of the Bosnian gangster and our psychic-psycho cousin Burt."

"Well, I hardly think she could get off on such a defense. Coercion defenses have been effective in some cases, but rarely. The more reasonable hope would be to convince the prosecution that she means to go to trial with that defense, in the hope that the prosecution might agree to some sort of plea bargain for a short prison term, or even probation, just to avoid what could turn out to be a lengthy, complicated trial. But it doesn't sound like her court-appointed lawyer is all that interested in making that sort of effort in this case. He obviously thinks the government has a slam dunk case and doesn't think it's worth fighting."

"Yeah, I agree. She did say she would love to get a private attorney to represent her, but Aunt Margaret didn't seem interested in helping out on that score."

Makelle picked up the envelope again and said, "Liverpool. I just left Liverpool, and I have to say I never had so much fun as I had this past year I spent there teaching." He looked over at Charlotte. "I wouldn't mind going back and spending a few more weeks there. Not as her attorney, of course; I'm not licensed to practice law there. But maybe we can help sort things out with Carolyn. But I'll go only if you come with me. I'm not the type to hold hands and let someone cry on my shoulder. What do you say we take a little vacation and give Carolyn a hand? I can't go home to San Francisco for another few months, until my tenants leave in September. And my conference at Princeton has another three days to go."

"Great! That's what I was hoping you'd say. Yes, yes, yes! I even hinted to Margaret that I might be able to talk you into coming over, and guess what? She recommended a great bed and breakfast right in the middle of town. Carolyn's staying at Margaret's house until her criminal case is resolved. Her bail terms require her to stay home; she can't go more than 50 feet away from the house or her monitoring bracelet will call the cops. Margaret's grandson Danilo—Burt and Irene's son—will live in the cottage in the backyard while he attends the University of Liverpool, at least during his freshman year. I'm sure that arrangement will feel pretty weird to Dani."

"Wonderful. Sounds like a plan. I can introduce you to Heike, and maybe we can meet my daughter. God, it sounds so strange to say those words!"

"I think the earliest we could leave would be the twelfth of June. I'll see what flights are available around that date."

CHAPTER FIVE:
RENDEZVOUS IN TRIESTE

"**M**on Dieu! At least you could have called or written to tell me when you would arrive! Dushan emailed me at the end of April to say you were on your way. That was a month ago! What happened? Did you get lost?"

Claude Prejean set down the take-out box of "pasta e fagioli" that he brought back to his office from his favorite Trieste restaurant. His young friend—a friend who last year saved his life after Claude's skiing accident in Utah—was sitting at Claude's own desk chatting up Claude's secretary. Danilo Sandor—whom Claude had not seen since Danilo left Claude's former office in Utah to return home and straighten up matters after his father's suicide—jumped up, and with a grin as wide as his face, ran up to Claude and gave him a long hug.

When Dani released Claude, he said, "Sorry about that, my friend. My schedule has been somewhat fluid during these past few months, as you might imagine. I decided to take a few detours instead of just driving straight to Trieste from Ljubljana. So many great sights to see. And college girls to talk to! School just got out, apparently, and they're everywhere!"

Claude returned his secretary's smile as she left the office, and then turned back to Dani. "Welcome to my new home, the Department of Mathematics and Geosciences at the University of Trieste. So, are you gonna stay for awhile? Let me show you our fair city, Trieste? What are your plans? Last I heard, you were in Ljubljana visiting your stepbrother's family. How did that go?"

"Whoa, whoa, one thing at a time. Answers in reverse order: Yes, I had a great time in Ljubljana visiting Dushan's family. It actually felt like they were my family, strangely enough. Second, my plan now is to make my way back to Liverpool after I hang with you for a bit. I can only stay a week here and then I'm off. My grandmother lives there and has offered to let me live in her backyard cottage while I'm enrolled in the university. Can you put me up, or do I have to spend my last euros on a hotel?"

Claude smiled. "Of course I can put you up. My apartment is pretty tiny, but there is a guest bedroom. Or if you prefer, the University has rooms available for short-term guests. Faculty housing is across the quad. I'll take the afternoon off and take you there."

When they walked in the front door of Claude's apartment, Dani looked around, smiled, and said to Claude, "Well, it looks a little better than that ski cabin we stayed in in Utah last year. I'll accept your offer."

Claude laughed and said, "Yes, it's somewhat more comfortable. And we won't have to eat only onions and potatoes; the fine city of Trieste has a lot to offer gastronomically speaking."

*   *   *

It was a little past nine o'clock when Claude and Dani decided to have dinner. They had been catching up with each other's lives as they strolled through the picturesque city of Trieste on that warm night in late May. When they sat down at their outdoor table, Claude was the first to speak. "I hope you realize what an amazing life you've led, especially during the past year or so. And now you're about to embark on a very different voyage—you'll be a college student in one of the most interesting cities in England. I've never been there but they tell me that Liverpool is fascinating—on the water, ethnically diverse, great academic reputation. Speaking of academics, you don't sound like you've entirely made up your mind about your studies."

Dani smiled and said, "I was never a great student, but I was a little better in the sciences than in the liberal arts. I kind of think geology might be the way to go. I did pretty well in my earth science class when I was a senior in high school. But I'll have to see."

"I do hope you find the field interesting. I've worked in the field my whole career and absolutely love it. If you do well your first year, we might think about a summer internship working on one of my company's projects here. As I told you in the email, my project involves limestone preservation from Trieste over to Slovenia and Croatia and down the Dalmatian Coast."

Dani hesitated before launching the next topic on his mind. He felt a little embarrassed to get too personal with Claude, but his feelings of affection for him outweighed his trepidation. *I'm entitled. Hell, I saved his life and took care of him during a Utah winter; besides I don't think he'll mind.* "Claude, I get a distinct loneliness vibe from you. Are you dating anyone? I realize your career has meant a lot of travel and short-term projects. Has it been difficult to find time to meet someone?" Dani worried that Claude was in danger of becoming a hermit.

Claude sighed and forced a smile. "I had a feeling you would ask. Meeting women has been very difficult, for three reasons. First, as you said, my jobs tend to be only a few years before I get transferred to a different project somewhere else in the world. Second, the coworkers in the kind of jobs I get are almost entirely men. The final reason is the work is exhausting and leaves me too tired to think about dating."

"Well, you mustn't let yourself give up on the idea. Something tells me you would love to be in a relationship. How old are you, 35?"

"Close, very close. I'm 36. My birthday is October 2." Claude smiled and even chuckled a little. "You sound like a newspaper relationship columnist. Maybe you can hook me up with one of those English 'birds' in Liverpool when I come up to visit you."

"Oh, you're thinking of coming up? I was sort of thinking of coming down to Trieste in December over winter break."

"We can do that, too. We have a long winter break here, also, and it goes through mid-January. So, let's do this—you come down in December and we'll go somewhere together."

*   *   *

The next five days were filled with sightseeing and Dani's observations of several of the projects Claude's university team was working on. Dani and Claude said their goodbyes on June 4, Dani drove to the Trieste airport, dropped off the rental car, and got on a Boeing 737 to London. When the plane landed, he turned his cell phone back on and saw he had an email from Dushan:

Cap'n Dante, it looks like you're going to have to put up with the "New Me" sooner than you thought. I'm headed your way in a couple days. I finished my citizenship applications in Belgrade and Ljubljana and am now a dual citizen. I have a brand-new EU Slovenian passport! Interestingly, I also have an almost-as-new Serbian passport! Which shall I use? Decisions, decisions. I guess I'd better come as a Slovenian; who knows what those Brits might think of a Serb coming to visit.

Anyway, here's the deal. It looks like Carolyn's legal case is heating up and her attorney wants us (me, my dad, and you) to make nice with the dude prosecuting the case, and maybe a judge or two. Your Granny Margaret appears to be the one pulling strings behind the scenes. Get this—Carolyn's cousin Charlotte (do you remember her? I do; pretty cool lady!) is coming over from New Jersey with **her** *cousin to act as an international "consultant" for Carolyn. Should be interesting! My dad and I will arrive in Liverpool on June 10. And guess where we're staying—that old B&B where Carolyn handed me over to Burt! I don't really remember the place, just little dream-like images. I hope to God you'll have arrived by then. I mean, come on, Captain, you've been on the road since the end of April. Time to get settled in your new digs. I'm jealous! Jealous, do you hear?*

Dushansky

CHAPTER SIX:
STRANGE BEDFELLOWS

Margaret Sandor was sitting on her back porch enjoying the summer weather, a warm May evening, rare for Liverpool. She had just returned from her late-afternoon tai chi class and was full of energy. She chuckled when she thought back to three years ago when she joined the class. The teacher was shocked after the class when Margaret told her she was 85 years old. The teacher's words still rang in Margaret's ears—"Well, I have to say, you're in better shape and have more coordination and energy than most of my students who are at least 20 years younger than you."

Now, at the ripe old age of 88, Margaret was one of the tai chi teacher's assistants. Margaret was an energetic, tall woman with green eyes and long salt-and-pepper grey hair that she wore long, bucking the trend among other older women who cut their hair short.

Among her other physical pursuits were yoga and folk dancing. She had been folk dancing—Greek, Slavic, Middle Eastern—since her early teens. Many of the adults in her extended Greek-Hungarian clan kept those dance traditions alive by teaching the dances to the younger generation. Margaret kept the traditions alive even longer—long after others her age gave up dancing due to various infirmities. Still, even though she was by far the oldest dancer in her family, she was so good that she had no trouble recruiting younger members and keeping the traditions alive.

One of those younger members of her folk dancing class back some 40 years ago was her second cousin Charlotte, who moved to Los Angeles after graduating college and marrying Greg Bekas, yet another second cousin from a different branch of the clan. Margaret corresponded regularly with Charlotte, but hadn't seen her since she and Greg moved away. Charlotte's latest letter was full of news about Charlotte's younger cousin Makelle Ringhiera, a lawyer from San

Francisco whose daughter lived in Liverpool. Margaret had never met Makelle but knew his mother Melina Bekas, Greg's younger sister, before she moved to Africa and met and married Makelle's father, a half-Eritrean, half-Italian man named Takeste Ringhiera.

Margaret was born Margaret Markos in 1926. Her parents and several uncles and aunts came to the UK in 1914 from Greece. Because her father and uncles were very protective and could not afford to pay a dowry to "marry her off," she remained single until she was almost 40. Her father finally arranged for her to marry a wealthy Hungarian emigré, Bruce Sandor, in 1965.

Bruce and his brother Dennis were sons of Bela Sandor, who Margaret later learned was most likely a Hungarian criminal or spy during World War II who was executed by the Soviets after the war. Margaret heard that the source of Bela's wealth came from a Hungarian bank he looted in the 1920's. Bela Sandor moved to the UK, set up a trust fund for his two sons and left the UK in the early 1940's when his wife died and London was being bombed relentlessly by the Nazis.

When Dennis reached adulthood and was able to access his share of the trust funds, he squandered most of his inheritance. He purchased a magnificent Liverpool mansion and turned it into an opulent bed and breakfast inn. But when he could not keep up with the mortgage, the inn was repossessed and he was forced to go to work. He got a job in a mine that a friend worked for. But his bad luck continued to haunt him, and he died soon afterwards in a mining accident.

Bruce was much more successful with his investments, but he died of lung cancer in 1977, leaving behind a very wealthy widow, Margaret, and their traumatized six-year-old son, Burt Sandor.

After Bruce died, Burt became a withdrawn, secretive child and teenager. Marriage to his second cousin Irene Argyris seemed to have calmed him down somewhat, as did Margaret's designating their two sons Dani and Markos as beneficiaries of her "Sandor Family Trust." But despite Burt's seeming good fortune in marriage and fatherhood, he remained psychically damaged by his father's death, and was distant towards Margaret even after his marriage. He had revered his father, and his death devastated Burt. Perhaps because Bruce and Uncle Dennis had been abandoned by their immigrant Hungarian father, Bela Sandor, Burt had developed a strong dislike towards immigrants.

Margaret never gave up on Burt, especially after his successes in college and marriage. He had stopped bad mouthing immigrants in his late teens, and seemed to have gotten over his former prejudices. But Margaret knew better than to attribute Burt's ostensible reformation to any attempt by her to "persuade" him to give it a rest. Margaret and her son shared an unusual mental gift, or curse, as the case may be. Each had a strong, innate, persuasive ability to influence others by using what Margaret called a "push" or "knack." Margaret learned early in Burt's teenage years that he was the more adept of the two in the persuasion department. During those years, every attempt of hers to influence him or persuade him to do something, or refrain from doing something, was met with a strong block by Burt, a mental push back that repulsed her suave prodding.

Because of her inheritance after her husband's death, Margaret never needed to work. But she always occupied herself with volunteering and charitable events. When British Prime Minister Thatcher came to power in 1979, Margaret became worried that the Conservative party would crack down on immigration. At age 53 Margaret became an ardent pro-immigrant activist and volunter. For the next 20 years she worked tirelessly for immigrant rights and welfare.

She retired in 1999 at age 73, a few weeks before her niece Carolyn disappeared. Margaret learned of Carolyn's illegal, "under the counter" adoption scheme shortly before then and was outraged. She had, of course, no idea that Carolyn's scheme would lead to the kidnapping of Dushan Sava from a Yugoslavian refugee, a kidnapping committed by Carolyn at Burt's urging.

One of Margaret's post-retirement goals was to redouble her efforts to bring together the Markos-Sandor clan, which consisted of her late brother-in-law Dennis's wife, the former Helena Markos, and their two children; Helena's brother David Markos and his wife Lisa Boudros; and the whole Argyris clan, Irene's people. Especially after Burt told Margaret of Irene's death, Margaret devoted a lot of energy to healing Irene's parents and siblings. Margaret had loved Irene, really loved her. She knew Irene from her childhood. After Dushan and Dani's recent surprise visit and departure for Slovenia, Margaret decided the Markos-Sandor-Boudros-Argyris clan would have to meet Dani. And Dushan, too, for that matter. She immediately recognized that Dani and Dushan had the same "knack" that Margaret and Burt had, even stronger. *But they need some training, some TLC, or else they might end up like my poor, misguided son.*

So, on this May evening in 2014, Margaret was examining her emotions and her plan, to see how they were getting along in her heart and mind. She wasn't sure her plan would work, but it sure would be satisfying to see all the players come together in a week or so to perform their assigned roles in Carolyn's criminal case. The first to arrive would be her grandson Dani Sandor. He was the "stepbrother" of Dushan, the boy Carolyn kidnapped and sold to Burt in San Francisco. *I wonder if Dushan still uses 'Sandor' or has taken up his real surname, 'Sava.'* Dani had phoned from Trieste to say he would arrive June 4.

Next to arrive would be Dushan and his father, coming at the request of Carolyn's defense attorney. They were supposed to arrive June 10. Marta, Dushan's mother, would not be able to come because she was taking her daughters to the Isle of Man to investigate a school for the girls. Finally, a few days after the arrival of Dushan and Dimitri, Charlotte Bekas and Makelle Ringhiera would show up. Charlotte was Carolyn's childhood friend and some kind of cousin; she had been married to Carolyn's late second cousin Gregory, from the Bekas branch of Margaret's extended clan. Makelle was Charlotte's childhood friend and nephew through his mother Melina Bekas. More important than his family connection, however, was the fact that Makelle was an international criminal lawyer.

Margaret was a little apprehensive about the next phase of her plan—to convince Dushan and Dimitri to help Carolyn avoid a prison term! She was afraid she wouldn't get far trying to evoke their sympathy for Carolyn by portraying her as a victim of Burt's powerful coercive powers, combined with her fear of that Balkan gangster who was after her. No, she would have to add something to the mix, and she believed she had just the right ingredient—the bond between Dani and Dushan. Margaret had gone over her lines in the scenario numerous times.

"Think about it—you two wouldn't be together, wouldn't even know each other, if it weren't for Carolyn. Forget about her own excuse for what she did; that's for the legal folks to sort out and evaluate. The key, as far as you two are concerned, is that you two grew up together as a direct result of what Carolyn did. If you, Dushan, are willing to tell the court you have forgiven her, it will most

likely have a powerful effect. And you, Dani, can attest to how you two grew up together in that sad family, victims of Burt's callous disregard for anyone but himself. I, Burt's mother, can confirm your description of Burt's controlling nature, and can explain the single most motivating factor in his behavior—the money in the Trust I set up for his children."

Margaret knew there was a weak part of her plan—Dushan's parents' reaction to it. Marta and Dimitri lost their son for virtually his entire childhood! The suffering they felt all those years must have been unimaginable! How could they be asked to forgive such an evil woman? Moreover, Dimitri and Marta's victimization was arguably more severe than Dushan's from a legal point of view, since they believed that in all likelihood their child was dead. Dushan's anguish was his separation from his parents, who he believed were still alive.

Still, if Margaret could enlist their support for—or at least, non-opposition to—her plan, their cooperation could be a powerful influence on the judge and prosecutor. She believed she had two arguments to present Dimitri and Marta with. First, as with what she would tell Dushan and Dani, was the incredible bond between the boys. That bond was just as relevant to Dimitri and Marta as it was to the boys themselves—a great love and friendship had grown up, and it was the direct result of Carolyn's weakness of character. Margaret knew, from talking to Dani on the phone after the family reunion in Ljubljana, that Dimitri and Marta were deeply impressed and moved by that bond between their son and his "stepbrother."

The second argument would involve Makelle and Charlotte. Margaret decided on this argument a few days ago, and called them yesterday. The germ of the idea occurred to her during a phone conversation she was having with Jaleh and Thomas Kilpatrick, the couple from the Isle of Man who had known Dimitri since before Dushan's kidnapping. Jaleh called to ask Margaret if she had any news from "the boys," as she called them. Margaret told her that she expected to see them in the next few weeks when they arrived. Jaleh's husband, Thomas, came on the line, and during their chat he, a commercial lawyer himself, commented on how fascinating he found international law to be. He and Jaleh also talked to Margaret about Dimitri's outrage over the suffering experienced by the refugees in the UK.

When Jaleh and Tom said that, Margaret immediately thought of Makelle—not as a possible defense attorney for Carolyn, because he was not a member of the English Bar. Instead, Margaret thought he might impress the government's attorney, and the judge, with his expertise on international child trafficking—which was after all how this case began. And Makelle having a daughter who lived in Liverpool might give him some sort of connection to Liverpool in the judge's eye. Of course, as such he might also impress Dimitri and Marta as someone who could do something about the shameful criminal exploitation of refugees in the British Isles, a phenomenon closely related to the child trafficking crisis.

The key to winning Dimitri and Marta's cooperation in Carolyn's defense could well be Margaret's idea of hunting down the Bosnian gangster who originally got Carolyn entangled in the illegal adoption scheme back in 1999. Makelle might be able to convince Carolyn, the prosecution, and Dimitri and Marta, that Carolyn's assistance in finding the mysterious "Mr. Aksoy" and his associates would be a tremendous boon to the plight of the British refugee community, not to mention a serious blow to the related criminal enterprises that Aksoy's organization had spawned here and elsewhere in Europe. Those criminal enterprises were even more widespread and active after the refugee flood from Syria and Libya began. Surely, the prosecution would look favorably on such information in deciding what sentence to recommend to the judge.

Margaret had tried several times to get Carolyn to talk about Aksoy, but she was so terrified of him that she would always cut the conversation short. After Margaret got to know Lieutenant Ailshie, the now-retired police inspector from Isle of Man who had worked on Dushan's kidnapping case for years, she got a little more information. Ailshie told Margaret about the legal mess Carolyn and her co-worker Derrick Nelson had gotten into after their illegal adoption business had been exposed in the beginning of 1999. When Ailshie began working with Dimitri in the kidnapping case, he interviewed Nelson after he had plea-bargained himself out of the pending illegal-adoption case. Ailshie had been hoping to learn more about Carolyn, especially her maiden name, which nobody seemed to know. But he had never thought to try to get more information about Aksoy.

After Dushan and Dani introduced Ailshie to Margaret last December, he told Margaret that he believed Nelson probably had known more about Aksoy, but had only given minimal information about him to the authorities; he was no doubt terrified of what Aksoy's people might do to him. Still, Margaret believed Carolyn could be persuaded to be forthcoming about Aksoy once she saw that that information might be critical to avoiding a prison term in her kidnapping case. Persuading her would be easier if Inspector Ailshie was successful in finding Nelson and talking him into cooperating in the hunt for Aksoy. Margaret's plan would start coming together, God willing, in less than a week, with the arrival of Dani.

Carolyn was already there, living in the guest bedroom in Margaret's house, nervously awaiting word from the Liverpool public defender's office telling her the date of her next court hearing or meeting with the prosecutor's office. No doubt about it, in Carolyn's view, Margaret had pulled a rabbit out of a hat when she talked the judge into releasing Carolyn on bail pending resolution of her criminal case. Of course, Carolyn now had to stay on the property at all times, wearing an electronic bracelet to ensure she didn't stray. She wasn't complaining, however. It was a hell of a lot better than her accommodations for the past six months or so—her Liverpool jail cell.

Margaret was looking forward to seeing Charlotte Bekas, a niece-by-marriage of one of Margaret's second cousins as well as a bona fide blood relative from another branch of the family. It had been decades since they last met, and Charlotte had been barely out of her twenties back then. Margaret was even more eager to once again meet Charlotte's exotic nephew, Makelle Ringhiera. Makelle was a Bekas on his mom's side, making him half Greek and a nephew of Charlotte's husband Greg. His father, Takeste Ringhiera, was half-Eritrean and half-Italian. Makelle was a respected law professor from California, who not only taught international criminal law, but also took on the occasional real case. That specialty and Carolyn's close relationship with Charlotte were two of the reasons for Margaret's hope that a favorable plea bargain could be had in Carolyn's case.

The other reasons were Dushan, his parents, and Dani, who might be persuaded that it was more important to cooperate in a concerted effort to find Aksoy and shut down his Europe-wide criminal enterprises, than to seek vengeance against Carolyn. *We shall see; we shall see.*

Margaret had only recently learned, several months earlier, that she had a partner in her campaign to "push" the boys and Dushan's parents into influencing Carolyn's case in a positive way. That partner, with whom she had only recently shared several dream encounters, was Dushan's great grandmother, Shimza. Margaret and Shimza had not actually met yet, at least not in person. But her awareness of Shimza first appeared in Margaret's mind back in February when Shimza met the boys at Marta and Dimitri's home in Ljubljana.

Margaret, of course, wasn't present at that family reunion; she was about a thousand miles away, in England, about to drop off to sleep. But a kind of connection happened. In Ljubljana, Shimza was lying in bed after Marta's welcoming party for the boys wound up for the night. She was reliving her first impression of Danilo, savoring the connection that she so strongly felt between Dani and Dushan. That's when she felt *another* connection, the connection to Dani's grandmother.

Margaret, in England, like Shimza in Ljubljana, was lying in bed. Margaret experienced a feeling of warmth in her chest that was accompanied by brightness around the periphery of her vision. It lasted not more than 10 or 15 seconds, and the name of Dushan's great grandmother shimmered through the haze—"**Shimza**." Margaret instantly remembered the term for the haze—"glamour"— a word from her childhood days when she would spend much of her free time reading and hearing about faeries and how they used glamour to disguise things or make things appear that would otherwise remain invisible. The glamour made Margaret smile, and she felt her smile fly back to Shimza in acknowledgment. Their minds stayed connected long enough to form this thought in unison—*We're "blood sisters" now; good things will happen!*

CHAPTER SEVEN:
A FORCE OF NATURE

Shimza awoke at five a.m. on her 85th birthday, June 12, 2014, glad to still be alive in good health despite her advanced age. In fact, she didn't feel anywhere near 85, and was always too embarrassed to tell anyone her true age; *I don't think they really believe me, so why bother?*

It was almost four months after her visit to the reunited family in Ljubljana. The dream was still with her, except she knew it wasn't entirely a dream. Ever since she "saw" her granddaughter Marta's pregnancy over 20 years ago, she had remained connected to her, Marta's husband Dimitri, baby Dushan in Marta's womb, and Marta's two daughters Aisha and Shimza born seven years later. Now, after the reunion in Ljubljana, Shimza's latest dream was triggered by her meeting Dushan's American "stepbrother" Danilo Sandor. *Two powerful adepts, those two!*

The dream began with scenes from her latest meeting with the Rom community leaders in Istanbul concerning her work in trying to resolve some of their difficulties related to homelessness and general economic discrimination in Turkey as well as all over Eastern Europe. The first part of the dream was simply a rehash of the meeting. But then it turned into something that didn't "happen," but was nonetheless understood by Shimza as a hint of things to come. A Rom woman asked, "How will you make your plan come about?" Shimza's dreaming mind understood that the plan the woman asked about wasn't the plan under discussion at the meeting, a plan concerning lease negotiations with the Istanbul municipality for a plot of land on the Asian side of the Strait, about 100 yards from the site of the proposed future Baha'i Temple. No, Shimza understood the woman to be asking about the "tapestry" being woven in Shimza's mind, a tapestry woven by her great-grandchildren, including a "step" great-grandchild she had only met recently, Danilo.

She loved the story of Dushan and Dani, who grew up together, Dani being a year older, in California. Shimza had dropped everything and returned to Ljubljana as soon as she heard that long-lost Dushan had shown up with his brand-new stepbrother Dani. It was a bit of a chore to postpone the things she had planned on doing in Istanbul in February, but on the other hand the weather in Istanbul was so unseasonably cold, especially in her tiny little apartment with only an ancient ceramic Turkish stove for heat, that she was relieved to be able to spend a little time in a warmer place and in a real house, a house full of family.

When Shimza arrived at the family home in Ljubljana, everyone was still in "reunion" mode. It became a full-fledged party with Shimza's arrival. Marta had told Shimza that she worried that the only two people who really had any memory of Shimza were herself and Dimitri. When Marta took her grandmother aside in the kitchen she remarked, "Ever since your unexpected visit to our honeymoon hotel in Niš almost 20 years ago, you only returned to Ljubljana twice, once when the twins were two years old, and again when they were five. I guess I'm wondering if in the eight years since then, the girls' memory of you has become more and more reliant on the stories Dimitri and I told them."

Marta was pleasantly surprised to see how quickly the girls proved her wrong. They ran to and embraced their "Nonna" Shimza with immediate recognition. Giggles and more hugs, and then the questions. From the girls: "Nonna, why didn't you come visit more often?" From Nonna: "Well, you know how busy people get, and besides we had our little dream visits, didn't we? You remember those."

Marta, of course, was overjoyed to see the girls hadn't forgotten their great grandmother. But still, she couldn't quite understand how they could have retained many memories of her over such a long span of time. Turning away from the girls' chattering with their Nonna, Marta was struck by the expressions on Dushan's and Dani's faces. They displayed none of the awkwardness of strangers waiting to be introduced to an ancient relative. No, they looked almost as overjoyed to see her as the girls.

For Nonna's part, the experience of meeting Dani created a feeling of warmth in her heart and a haze at the periphery of her vision. It reminded her of the glamour she used to hear the Rom elders talk about, a way to distinguish friend from enemy in the larger communities they found themselves in. She was something of an adept herself. *It's a good knack to have, that's for sure.* But she remembered when she was a teenager and had not been trained yet; she was frightened by her ability to "see" people's emotions. She was shocked to hear the elders use the term glamour in this way. She had only heard the term used in children's stories, where the faery folk would use their glamour to make themselves invisible. When she asked whether they were talking about the same thing, an elder set her straight. "Not the same thing, but related, yes, related. Some people can develop such sensitivity, but not to the degree the Fae have developed. We are not like the Fae, who came before us."

When Shimza lay in her bed that evening, she recalled the glamour she felt when as she shook Dani's hand. Although she instantly recognized the haze in her eyes as a glamour, she was not sure why it occurred in that moment. *I certainly wasn't creating the glamour. Was Dani? Was he aware of it?*

She kept rolling those thoughts around in her mind as she drifted off to sleep, except it was conscious sleep, a lucid dream of sorts. She held the glamour in her dream hands as if it were a globe and passed it through a gauze veil to Dani's grandmother, Margaret. Shimza had never met Margaret; in her dream she used the glamour to introduce herself to Margaret. Within a few seconds, Shimza saw Margaret smile in response as she passed the globe back to Shimza. As the globe paused between them, their minds acknowledged each other. Shimza saw faces in the globe. Three she recognized—Dani, Dushan and Carolyn, the woman who had kidnapped Dushan. The fourth face was that of a man Shimza didn't recognize. *All in good time, all in good time,* her dream voice said as she drifted into a deeper sleep in which she entered the dream of the Rom conference.

Now, four months later, as Shimza got out of bed in her old Istanbul apartment, she recalled the two dreams. She realized that her memory of the two stepbrothers, and the glamour she and Margaret exchanged, were what triggered her dream of the Rom conference. The dream seemed to be telling her that those young men were somehow destined to play a part in her as-yet not fully developed plan for the Rom people. She originally conceived of her plan, still very vague, when her husband, Tomas Cecelja, died in 1977. When that happened, Shimza decided to leave Ljubljana and move to Bulgaria in the hope that living in an ancient Rom community would help her vague ideas take a more concrete shape.

Shimza was 50 when she moved to Bulgaria two years later, and 65 when she moved to Istanbul looking for even greater involvement in the well-established Rom community there.

Now, 20 years after her arrival in Istanbul (and still looking the same age as when she arrived), she had two immediate tasks to complete. The first was to finish up the outline for the lectures she was scheduled to give during her final seminar at Bosporus University. The second task was to make a reservation for her flight to Liverpool in mid-June. Dani's grandmother Margaret offered to meet her at the airport and drive her to the B & B she had booked for her. Danilo should have returned to Liverpool by then from his visit with his friend Claude in Italy. Before starting as a college student at Liverpool University, Dani would most likely be testifying in Carolyn's criminal case. Shimza knew that the strong bond between Dani and Dushan would play a role in Carolyn's case.

After her arrival in Liverpool, Shimza was to meet with the director of the Liverpool Rom program. She also had an appointment with the headmaster of St. Ninian's, the secondary school Marta and Dimitri hoped to enroll their daughters in.

CHAPTER EIGHT:
LOOKING FOR JUSTICE

On June 5, the day after he arrived in Liverpool, Dani felt on top of the world. To begin with, he woke up full of energy and enthusiasm in his Grandma Margaret's beautiful little cottage in her backyard after a restful sleep. His flight from Trieste had been long, including a three-hour wait at Heathrow for his connecting flight to Liverpool, and his arrival was late in the evening. His grandmother showed him the cottage almost immediately, without lingering in the house itself. *If I didn't know better, I'd say she didn't want me to stick around in the house any longer than necessary.* Dani had a feeling Carolyn was sleeping in the guest bedroom in the house. But he didn't ask; he was too tired and looking forward to getting some shuteye after his long days and late nights carousing with Claude and his buddies in Trieste for the past week.

His suspicions were confirmed the next morning when he dressed and went outside to take in the glorious day. Carolyn was sitting in a lawn chair next to the little vegetable garden, reading a book. Looking up, she said to Dani, "Well, we might as well get the awkwardness over with. Remember me? I'm Carolyn Markos Owens, the evil witch who kidnapped your stepbrother." She stood and offered her hand. Dani, feeling more than a little flustered, hesitated, but then stepped forward. But he didn't take Carolyn's hand.

Dani stepped back and said, "Of course I remember you; we're family. My dad's cousin, right? But we have a big problem, don't we? A big, complicated problem. I'm here for two reasons—I'm gonna start college in a couple of months; and I'm going to testify in your kidnapping case. See what I mean about complicated? It has been a long, long time, Carolyn... but I'm not prepared to say that what you did is water under the bridge."

Just the barest hint of a frown passed over Carolyn's face, and then she said, "Well, let's start at the beginning. Has your grandmother caught you up on matters? How do you like my little charm bracelet here?" Carolyn raised her left arm to show off the little electronic monitoring bracelet for Dani.

Dani didn't answer for a few moments. Instead, he let his emotions catch up with his mind as he looked around at the garden and the hedges that fenced in Margaret's backyard. Then he turned back to Carolyn. "Yes, I'm pretty caught up on matters. You were finally apprehended some months back, after being on the run for what, 10 or 12 years?"

"Something like that. Most of that time I lived in the States and Canada. It was only when I had to return to the UK that things caught up with me."

Dani grimaced at Carolyn's use of the phrase "had to return." "It sounds like you admit that your return to the UK was more out of necessity than your own sense of justice. Let's face it. You couldn't live with yourself, but at the same time you were in full fugitive mode; am I right? Which was the dominating motivation—your survival sense or your moral sense? Correct me if I'm wrong, but I think survival trumped. It was only after your arrest that you started trying to convince yourself that you wanted to return to make things better for everyone."

Dani's speech left him a little breathless, agitated, almost angry. He could see Carolyn's tears leaking out of her eyes. But he waited to hear her actually express her agreement in words.

"I wanted to set things right, Dani. That's the truth, the very truth; God's truth. I wanted to pay for what I did. When I decided to come back home, you're right—at first I still felt like a fugitive, I wanted to stay out of sight. But once I left Canada on the ship, it was like a dark cloud broke over me. I expected a storm, but instead it was relief. I wanted to get all this behind me, make it better for everyone. I'm ready for whatever happens to me, Dani. What gives me greatest comfort is seeing that the evil thing I did has resulted in a happier ending than anyone could have imagined; at least happier than the alternative. I hope and pray that you, Dushan, his family and everyone else can eventually forgive me, Dani, I really mean that."

Dani doubted that Carolyn had truly been ready to turn herself in, since she had stayed out of sight for a long time after her arrival in England. And she had **not** turned herself in at all—it was the police who found her after Margaret alerted them to her whereabouts. He also doubted Carolyn was "ready for whatever happens" to her, including a prison term. Her fear of that possibility was obvious. But then he sighed and said, "I don't know what Dushan's reaction will be, or his father's. I don't even know how I feel, but if the judge asks me about our family life, I'll tell the truth. That's all I can say."

Dani turned and walked away from Carolyn before she could respond. He took advantage of the rest of that fine June day to do a little sightseeing in Liverpool. The next day, the 6th, he went over to the university to check on the status of his admission. His grandmother had set things up so that all he had to do was complete and sign the formal application and some other paperwork. Although Margaret had pulled a few strings to allow his application to proceed, even though well past the deadline, she didn't pay any of the costs and fees. But that didn't bother Dani in the least. *Not to worry. She knows that this rich boy can cover the tab! Some of the money came from her, anyway.* Dani spent the better part of the afternoon poring over the class catalog and working out some semblance of a schedule.

The university was so sprawling and rich in its grounds and architecture that Dani decided to come back the next day and do a proper tour. That night, however, still full of energy and stimulated by all that he was seeing, he decided to check out one of the many and varied music venues in the city. The one he chose had an interesting band playing that night, a gypsy group called the 'Roman Candles.' His grandmother had told him that a grand-niece of hers played in that band. There were five in the band—a tall Middle Eastern-looking man doubling on clarinet and soprano sax; a short Asiatic-looking guy playing an electric bass; a short Gallic-looking guy with a wild head of red hair playing a violin; a tall African-looking man playing a box drum called a "cajon;" and a tall, Mediterranean-looking woman with dreadlocks playing a stringed instrument that looked sort of like a guitar. "She must be Jaelle," Dani said aloud as found a table near the front. They all looked to be in their thirties. They played a lively mix of funk, klezmer, and eastern European gypsy stuff.

During the band's break, Dani took the opportunity to ask the woman band member about her instrument; he was a little nervous about introducing himself. She looked at Dani for a moment before smiling and said, "It's called a 'bouzouki.' It's probably Greek originally, but lots of different bands feature it—gypsy, Irish, you name it." Dani thought he detected just a trace of a German accent.

Pointing to another stringed instrument on its stand on the stage, Dani asked, "And what about that other guitar-looking instrument up there. You haven't played that one yet. I've never seen a guitar with no frets and the tuning head bent backwards 90 degrees."

"It's called an 'oud.' It's Arabic, Turkish, Greek, Armenian, they all use it in their music. The Greek version is called 'lauto.' Just wait til our second set; you'll love the sound."

Feeling a lot more confident, Dani extended his hand and said, "By the way, I'm Danilo Sandor. Do you happen to be Jaelle Ringhiera?"

She smiled, shook his hand and said, "One and the same. Pleased to meet you. How do you know my name?"

He felt a tingling in his chest from their handshake that distracted Dani for a moment. "When I told my grandmother I would probably go see some live music tonight, she told me to look you up here. She says we're distant cousins. Don't ask me how. I just arrived from Ljubljana. I'm gonna start my freshman year at the university."

"Ljubljana? That's a very pretty city, the old part at least. I've actually been there, on a trip with my mom. We're German, mostly. But you're not Slovenian; your accent is 100% American and your last name sounds Hungarian. Your grandmother wouldn't by any chance be Margaret Sandor?"

"Yes she is. So, yes, I'm part Hungarian. As well as American, Greek and English. I was visiting some family in Ljubljana, which as you say is beautiful. Now I'm staying with my grandmother here in Liverpool while I get things together to start school." Dani half-smiled at Jaelle and said, "You said you're German 'mostly.' What's the rest? You look a little Mediterranean and maybe East African. And your name, Ringhiera, sounds Italian."

"I am 'all of the above,' as you Americans say. I'm partly Rom and German on my mom's side, and Italian, Greek and Ethiopian on my father's side."

"Cool. That mixture certainly shows up in your music. Do you and the band have a lot of gigs in Liverpool? Some of my family will be arriving soon for a visit and I'd love to take them out to one of your concerts."

"Not as many as we would like, especially not as the Roman

Candles playing our gypsy stuff. But we play at this club on Fridays and Saturdays. We're all in other bands and have various gigs separately other nights of the week. We have a website where you can check out our various schedules, or book us for a gig!" Jaelle handed Dani her card, a colorful card with the band's name, the website, and her name, Jaelle Ringhiera, superimposed over what looked like the Roman Coliseum in the background. She added, "But if you wait too long, we—or at least I—may be playing in another band in a different city. I've been in contact with several touring bands, so we'll see what happens."

Putting the card in his wallet, Dani smiled and said, "I'll definitely check out your schedule and try to come back."

"That would be great. Well, I've got to get a drink before the break's over. Stick around and enjoy the second set."

CHAPTER NINE:
A BREAKFAST TO REMEMBER

Charlotte and Makelle were very impressed with the beauty and comfort of the bed and breakfast inn Margaret had booked them in. They checked into their rooms at 4:30 on June 12 and strolled around the inn's two floors. The proprietress was out and had texted them the front-door code and left their room keys in an envelope just inside the front door with a note: "Please make yourselves at home. I'll be back this evening around 9 p.m. to drop off some breakfast supplies. I will return with our cook tomorrow morning well before breakfast, which is from 8 to 10 a.m. The doors to the other two rooms are closed because the other guests have checked in already. Enjoy your evening. I've put a list of recommended restaurants and pubs on the dining table."

Charlotte walked around the dining room, admiring the expensive period furniture, then walked through the large kitchen. "Wow; this place is the real deal, Makelle. Who was it that Margaret said turned this into a bed and breakfast?"

"One of her late husband's brothers, or uncles, I forget. I wonder who the other guests are. I've always loved sitting down to breakfast with fellow tourists, haven't you?"

"Yeah, it's one of my guilty pleasures. Some people can't stand to have to make conversation with strangers, but I don't mind at all. At the very least you can talk about the wonderful food and interesting sights to see in the city."

It was still early in the day, especially in those northern latitudes where it didn't get dark until after 10 o'clock in the summer. They decided to walk around the city a bit to work up an appetite.

The next morning they went downstairs for breakfast at 8 a.m. The other guests were already seated at the table. Two of the guests were a dark-haired Slavic-looking man who looked to be in his late forties and a young man who looked to be in his late teens or early twenties; they looked like they could be father and son. The other two guests were apparently a couple. Charlotte thought the husband looked Irish and the wife looked Middle Eastern. The four of them were chatting away happily, as if they had known each other for a long time. A middle-aged woman, perhaps the proprietress, was smiling and chatting with the guests as she placed the platters of breakfast items on the table.

Everyone at the table looked up when Charlotte and Makelle entered the room. Makelle was the first to speak. "Good morning, everyone! I'm Makelle and this is Charlotte."

Before Charlotte could speak, the young man at the table spoke up. "Charlotte! I can't believe it. I recognize you from a long time ago in California. Am I right?"

Charlotte stared at the young man, who was getting up from the table. Then something clicked in her head and she smiled. "Could it be? Are you Dushan Sandor?"

Dushan walked up to her and they hugged. Dushan took a step back and said, "I USED to be Dushan Sandor. Now I'm Dushan Sava. This is my dad, Dimitri Sava." Dimitri, who along with everyone else at the table had arisen, said, "Pleased to meet you, Charlotte. I'm afraid I am a little lost. My son hasn't mentioned anyone named Charlotte."

Dushan turned to Charlotte as if to invite her to answer the question. She said to Dimitri, "Frankly, I'm a little surprised that he would remember me. I only used to see him and his stepbrother Danilo occasionally when they were little boys. I stopped visiting after a few years." Charlotte paused to gauge Dimitri's reaction. Then she shook his hand and continued. "Mr. Sava, I have only recently learned the truth about Dushan's kidnapping and I have to say I'm still in shock. What a terrible thing that was."

At this point, the Middle-Eastern-looking woman said, "Why don't we all introduce each other and get back to our delicious breakfast before it gets cold? I'm Jaleh Kilpatrick and this is my husband Thomas."

Thomas smiled, shook everyone's hand and said, "Pleased to meet you, Charlotte and Makelle. Jaleh and I have known Dimitri and his son for quite some time, both before and after Dushan's kidnapping." Gesturing at the delicious food on the table, Thomas added, "Now, let's tuck in!"

For the next few minutes, their conversation was intermittent and casual as they ate breakfast. Dushan turned to Makelle and said, "I'm curious as to why you and Charlotte are here. I seem to remember that Charlotte, my so-called 'step mom' Irene, and Carolyn were cousins and originally came from England."

Makelle looked at Charlotte, who nodded her head slightly. Then he said to Dushan, "I'm Charlotte's nephew; actually her late husband's nephew. Charlotte's husband was Gregory Bekas, my mom's cousin. He was also Carolyn's cousin. I could spend all day filling you in on my convoluted background and how I fit into this crazy-quilt family. But back to your question—I'm showing Charlotte around Liverpool, where I recently finished a yearlong teaching gig at Liverpool University teaching international criminal law. We're also here on 'business,' in a manner of speaking."

Thomas spoke next. "Dushan, you recall when you, Dani and Inspector Ailshe met Dani's grandmother, Margaret Sandor last December? Well, after that meeting, Margaret assisted Inspector Ailshie in locating Carolyn and arranging for her arrest on the kidnapping charge. Carolyn has been charged and has only recently been released on bail, awaiting her trial."

Dushan poured himself another cup of coffee and said to Makelle, "So, is her case the 'business' you spoke of?"

"Yes, but only indirectly. That's why we're all here. You and your dad, too, obviously. Everyone has some interest in this case."

"But what's your interest in this case?" Dushan's voice was a little tight, and his face registered a look of concern. Dimitri noticed the change in Dushan's demeanor and said to Makelle, "You say you're a lawyer. Are you here to help Carolyn?"

The room became very quiet. Makelle took a sip of coffee, put down the cup and addressed Dimitri directly. "Not at all. My interest in the case is the illicit so-called 'adoption' of refugee children all over the UK and Europe. My more specific interest is the smuggling ring allegedly operated by a certain Bosnian fellow named Bulent Aksoy. It seems that our relative Carolyn got herself tangled up in one of Aksoy's schemes back in the late 90's and got in a lot of trouble; not to mention the heartache she caused when she kidnapped your son."

At this, the silence in the room became even quieter. A few heartbeats later, Dimitri responded. "For a moment, I thought you were going to say you were going to help Carolyn, or act as her attorney. So, that is not what you're here for?"

"I'm not going to represent or counsel her, no. I'm not licensed to practice law in the United Kingdom, Mr. Sava, or anywhere outside the State of California. I'm a law professor, primarily, and my particular interest is the international abduction and smuggling of refugee children. That smuggling no longer comes from the former Yugoslavian republics, which used to be the primary phenomenon. Now most the victims come from the Middle East and North Africa, such as Syria and Libya."

Dushan spoke up. "I think I'm beginning to see how your interest might be relevant here. I mean, we're obviously all here to see that the prosecution's case against Carolyn is as strong as possible. My dad and I are direct victims of her crime. Jaleh and Tom are witnesses as well, though not as direct. And I suppose, since you're not here to represent Carolyn in court, you must be hoping to get her to help you find and shut down Mr. Aksoy. Does that sound about right?"

Makelle smiled and said, "Very astute. And, as you might be wondering, convincing her to give up information on Aksoy will be very, very difficult. It will be a miracle if she decides to help the authorities find him. You see, I've learned from her Aunt Margaret, Danilo's grandmother, that Carolyn is deathly afraid of Aksoy. Even if she knows how to find him, it's possible she would never consider providing that information to the government, especially since her cooperation might not help her get a reduced prison sentence."

Jaleh took advantage of the next few moments of silence to add some new information to the mix. "If I may, I think I have an interesting bit of information here. When last I spoke with Inspector Ailshie—my good friend Angus from all these years since he began the investigation into Dushan's kidnapping—he and I discussed an intriguing approach to finding Mr. Aksoy. Even if Carolyn refuses to cooperate in offering up any information—and I might add even if her former partner-in-crime Mr. Derrick Nelson also pretends ignorance—there may be another way to find Aksoy."

Makelle put down his glass of orange juice and said, "Any avenues leading to his arrest are obviously worthy of exploration. I would love to meet the Inspector."

Jaleh smiled and said, "Oh, I'm sure he would love to meet you as well. Here's the idea he and I came up with. Dimitri and Dushan know that I'm a member of the British Isles Baha'i Cluster, a loose association of the many small Baha'i communities in the UK and its crown protectorates. Many of us are former citizens of Iran who fled that merciless and cruel regime after the mullahs overthrew the Shah in the late 1970's. Many of the Iranian expats who fled to Europe and America—including the Iranian Baha'is—were eventually granted refugee status based on religious persecution.

"Before that status was bestowed on them by the British and other European governments, however, some of them were approached by scoundrels like Bulent Aksoy offering a variety of illegal or at least questionable proposals to help them financially. Aksoy's current victims come from the massive wave of refugees flooding Europe from Syria and North Africa. One of the most heartless of his schemes is to offer them temporary foster care for their children while the parents find jobs and housing. In reality, however, Aksoy and his organization actually sell the children to childless single people who believe they are adopting them. Even if some of those people become dissatisfied with the 'adopted' child and decide to return him or her, when they contact Aksoy or his organization they are told to deliver the child to a specified foster agency. When that happens, of course, the agency knows nothing of the so-called adoption, and calls the police. Eventually, the child **may** be reunited with the parent, but Aksoy cannot be found."

Makelle raised his eyebrows and said, "So you think some of those folks might have bits and pieces of information on Aksoy. Yes, I see how that might lead to something. In fact, during my stint at L.U. this past year, I worked with an administrative assistant of Persian descent. She provided me with lots of background information on the various refugee support groups active on the Continent, especially Paris. Paris was her first stop in her own refugee experience fleeing Iran. She may even be a Baha'i; I never asked. I will definitely contact her soon. Either she or some of the people she met in her work might have heard of Aksoy."

Charlotte got up from the table and said, "Well, I for one have to get some fresh air. Just an FYI to everyone: Makelle and I are supposed to meet with Margaret and Carolyn this afternoon at Margaret's house. What about the rest of you?"

Dushan spoke up, "Me and my dad are footloose today; nothing on the schedule. Jaleh and Tom are headed over today to Angus Ailshie's place here in Liverpool. I don't quite know what's on my schedule after that. My dad and I are staying one more night here, and then perhaps Angus will invite us to stay at his place. Either today or tomorrow I'm hoping to see Dani, my stepbrother, and talk him into showing us around Liverpool a bit, even though he's only been here a week or so." Turning to Jaleh and Tom, Dushan asked, "Where are you staying after your visit with Angus?"

"I have a sister in Liverpool who said she can put us up starting tonight, so we'll do that," Tom said as he got up from the table. "I'll leave you her phone number so we can stay in touch. We have Angus's number already, so one way or another, we won't lose track of one another."

CHAPTER TEN:
MEETING WITH CAROLYN

Dushan's call surprised Dani just as he was preparing to leave Margaret's little backyard cottage for the day. *"Lucky I didn't plan on sleeping in this morning,"* he mumbled as he picked up his phone and shoved his laptop into his rucksack. It was when he checked the time on his phone that he saw that it wasn't morning at all—it was almost one o'clock in the afternoon. He grabbed his windbreaker and stepped outside. Dushan had given him a heads-up that Charlotte and Makelle were on their way to meet with Carolyn, and advised Dani to make himself scarce for the rest of the day; perhaps he could hook up with him and his dad.

When Dani learned that Tom and Jaleh were going to spend the day at Angus's place, he decided to invite himself to tag along. Maybe ask Dushan and Dimitri to go with him. *We'll see what Dushanski wants to do.* He walked out of Margaret's backyard and exited the property through the little gate on the side of the house, so as to avoid running into Carolyn inside the house. As he stood at the curb studying the Liverpool Metro phone app to figure out how to get to Angus's street, Dani saw a car turn the corner to his right. He worried that it might be Charlotte in the driver's seat, so he made a quick turn to the left and began walking briskly away from the house, hoping Charlotte had not seen him.

She hadn't. She was too busy trying to remember to stay on the left side of the road, while at the same time thinking about Makelle's and Jaleh's descriptions of the types of crimes people like Bulent Aksoy were involved in. Charlotte stopped in front of the house and said, "Okay, now the fun begins. I have absolutely no idea how this will turn out. But the thing we have to impress upon Carolyn is that if she hopes to avoid a lengthy prison term, she will have to provide important information to the government. You'll have to stress that what Aksoy was involved back in 1999 was small potatoes compared to what he's allegedly doing these days."

They got out of the car and began walking up the walkway to Margaret's front door. Makelle turned and said to Charlotte, "Not only that, but she may not even have to testify against him; if she can help the authorities find out where he operates, they may be able to set up a sting and arrest him for his current activities rather than what he was doing 15 years ago."

Charlotte looked skeptical. "But even if she gives us all the information we want, I still don't know how the prosecutor and the court will weigh that against the harm she did to Dushan and his family. That's a big problem, it seems to me. The way the government feels about Carolyn will be a big factor—if the prosecutor or judge is in a vindictive mood, I doubt that anything Carolyn says will count for much in their eyes." Makelle had no reply.

It was Carolyn who answered Charlotte's knock on the door and welcomed them to Margaret's home. She explained that Margaret had left on an errand a few hours ago and would return shortly. Carolyn showed them into the living room and they all sat down. Charlotte introduced Makelle to Carolyn, who thanked him for any help he could provide.

"I'm not sure I can provide much help, if any, Carolyn. I suspect that the only hope for you being able to avoid a long prison term would depend on how useful you might be in the government's eyes."

"I'm not sure I understand you. You don't think I can persuade them that I was basically coerced into an impossible situation?"

"No, even if you could convince them that Burt was some kind of mental freak, I doubt they would believe you had no defense to it. That would certainly take more than just your word. What I think might most impress the prosecution, and the court, would be the quality of the information you can provide them concerning the nature of the criminal organization that you became part of. And I stress the word 'might;' what I have in mind is a gamble." Makelle said nothing about how Dushan and Dimitri might view Carolyn's cooperation with the prosecution, or whether they would confirm her description of Burt's controlling personality.

Before Carolyn could respond, Charlotte said, "I think I hear a car pulling into the driveway." Carolyn stood and went to the window.

"Yes, Aunt Margaret has returned." Carolyn opened the door, greeted Margaret, and introduced her to their guests. After shaking hands with Makelle and hugging Charlotte, Margaret set her coat on the chair in the hall, walked to the sofa and sat down. "So, I get to meet the famous Makelle Ringhiera. Carolyn, has Charlotte filled you in on our famous relative?"

"Not really, other than telling me that he is a law professor from San Francisco and just completed a year-long course at the university here. We were just beginning to talk about my case when you arrived."

"Well, I see I haven't missed anything. I have a general idea of what Makelle's going to suggest. And I think it's a great idea. But instead of having that discussion here, might I suggest we do so over at my friend Angus Ailshie's place? It's not far from here, and his two visitors have an exciting idea Carolyn might want to consider. Plus, Angus himself has a little surprise for us, and lunch as well. My car's warmed up and rarin' to go, as the Americans say."

The "errand" Margaret had attended to earlier was a meeting at Angus's home in Walton, a district of Liverpool not far from Margaret's home in the Aintree district. She had driven over there as soon as Angus told her about his special visitor, Derrick Nelson. Angus had said, "You see, Margaret, when I rang up Nelson a few days ago I told him of my recent discovery that he had not been completely forthcoming during his plea negotiations regarding the scheme he and Carolyn were involved in with Mr. Aksoy. Of course he vigorously denied withholding any pertinent information. I said, 'you mean such as Aksoy's full name and the name of the little pub he owned in Liverpool, the place where you first met?' I tell you, Margaret, the moment of silence was priceless. I could tell that he was torn between demanding I tell him how I got hold of that information and pretending complete ignorance. Before he could make up his mind what to say, I suggested he join us for lunch at my home today, since he now lived in Liverpool. I think you should come over ASAP so you can meet him and we can have a little discussion. He doesn't know that we're not really sure about the name of Aksoy's pub; we've only heard scuttlebutt from our informants. But we'll play with Nelson and see what comes out."

That was exactly what Margaret did. When she arrived at Angus's home, Angus was serving tea to Nelson and the Kilpatricks, who had apparently only just arrived themselves. The "discussion" was short and took almost all of Margaret's considerable persuasive ability to get Derrick to help them out. "Mr. Nelson, let me assure you we're not interested in dragging you back into a court hearing to determine whether you lied during your plea negotiations all those years ago. We—that is, Inspector Ailshie and I and a few other people—believe you want to avoid that. All we want from you and Carolyn is confirmation that what you two tell us is the truth."

Derrick frowned. "Carolyn! Are you talking about Carolyn Owens? She's back?"

"Actually, she's better known these days as Carolyn Markos Owens, recently arrived from Canada, and America before that. She's my niece. She spent the last six months as a guest of the Liverpool city jail and is currently out on bail living at my home. She wears an electronic bracelet to ensure she doesn't stray. Our dear retired policeman Angus here has gotten permission from the Liverpool probation department for Carolyn to travel from my house to his house for the day."

Margaret could see the little wheels in Nelson's brain turning as he tried to figure out what exactly she meant by wanting them to "confirm" each other's information. She replied to his as-yet unspoken question. "I think you'll find the process easy enough. We've invited her and a couple of my relatives over here for afternoon tea. It will be a non-threatening meeting and in all likelihood a very short one."

Derrick resumed breathing, and after a short hesitation asked, "The Inspector told me you're after that Bosnian gangster I introduced to Carolyn, and that you think he might still be operating in a certain Liverpool pub. I have to say, Mrs. Sandor, the chances of him still being around, let alone alive, are slim to none."

At this point, Jaleh spoke up. "Excuse me, Mr. Nelson, but I can assure you Aksoy's still very much 'around;' he has had a very successful criminal career these past 20 years or so."

Nelson looked skeptical, and wondered how much this Middle-Eastern-looking woman knew. "Well, even if he's still around and running his criminal enterprise, how will you know if Carolyn's information is the truth? You're expecting me to confirm what she says, and her to confirm what I say, but you're assuming we know the truth about him, or that we won't deceive you."

As Margaret smiled and sipped her tea, Angus spoke up. "You don't need to worry about that, Mr. Nelson. That won't be a problem."

After that, Margaret returned to her home and brought Carolyn, Makelle and Charlotte back to Angus's home. At first, when Nelson heard the doorbell, his level of apprehension was fairly high. But as Margaret introduced everyone, he felt an almost immediate sense of calm, even when he shook hands with Carolyn, whom he had not seen (nor wanted to see) for almost 15 years. After the introductions the group sat down to the very substantial "tea" Angus had set out in his dining room. The group mostly chatted as they ate; nobody seemed to want to bring up an unpleasant subject.

As if being prompted, Carolyn felt she had to talk to Ailshie. "Angus, this is very difficult for me. I'm very sorry about what I did, and all the anguish I caused the boy and his family. It was a monstrous deed; I admit that. I was not myself; I felt like I was being forced into an impossible situation—Aksoy threatening me on one hand and Burt using his powers of psychic coercion on me on the other. I spoke with Dani yesterday and we had a talk about the situation. I explained to him how I felt, how what I did has been torturing me all these years. I hope he understood how I felt and still feel. I'm here to try to do what I can to help."

As Margaret listened to Carolyn, it occurred to her that Dimitri and Dushan were going to arrive momentarily, not only they but Dani as well. *Well, I hadn't counted on that, but I think this might be interesting.*

Angus noticed Margaret's distraction and glanced at her, trying to decide whether to respond to Carolyn's statement or let Margaret respond. Immediately, however, the doorbell rang. Angus got up, walked to the door and opened it. "Dimitri, my old friend! I wasn't expecting you, but I'm glad you're here. And Dushan and Dani couldn't resist coming along! Welcome, welcome."

Dimitri hugged Angus, and Dani and Dushan did the same. As the threesome walked into the entryway Dimitri said to Angus, "We had a feeling you might be having a party without us, so we decided to crash it. Any food left, or did you eat it all?"

"No, there's plenty left; we've hardly started. Come and join us. Help yourself at the buffet. Dushan and Dani, you two don't look like you're starving, so let Dimitri go first!"

When Dimitri and the boys walked into the dining room, they were visibly surprised to see Carolyn. Before they could speak, Margaret walked up to them and greeted them. Turning to Dani, she said, "I didn't want to wake you this morning so I let you sleep in. But I had no idea you would be coming."

Dani said, "I didn't know what was on my agenda for today, but when Dushan told me your relatives from the States would be here, I wanted to meet them." Dani walked over to Charlotte and Makelle and introduced himself. Margaret motioned for Dani, Dimitri and Dushan to come over and be introduced to Nelson. "This is Mr. Derrick Nelson, a former colleague of my niece Carolyn's." Nelson rose and shook hands with Dimitri, Dushan and Dani. "Pleasure to meet you. I'm almost as surprised as you to see this collection of people. But I'm told we will soon find out why we're here."

Angus said to Dimitri and the boys, "Please, help yourselves to some food and join us in the living room."

As they ate and chatted, the two stepbrothers became aware of Margaret's "focus" on them, which caused a tingling in their chests. They understood what she wanted—to keep an open mind once the discussion began. Dushan, who knew more of what Charlotte and Makelle had in mind, let Dani know to follow their lead at first. His glance at Dani said it all—*We'll play Margaret's trump card; watch and learn, Cap'n!*

Once his guests had finished eating, Angus said, "I want to make sure everyone knows why Margaret and I invited you to this meeting. We want to help out in a little house cleaning in the UK and beyond. We think we know a good place to start, and that's by tracking down one of the worst human traffickers in Europe, Bulent Aksoy. I think you all know about him, based on our previous discussions. I'll let Margaret elaborate a little bit on how we, as a group, can contribute to the effort to find him and shut him down."

Margaret, who had remained standing beside Carolyn's chair, smiled at everyone and began speaking. "We have a very special constellation of people here today, I hope you realize. I think I'm related to almost half of you. Let's see—Charlotte and Makelle, my niece and nephew, or grand-niece and grand-nephew, from the United States; my niece Carolyn Markos Owens, who now lives in Liverpool as a guest of our fair city's probation department; my grandson Danilo Sandor, who used to live in California; his so-called 'stepbrother' Dushan Sava and his father Dimitri, from Slovenia; Dimitri's good friends Tom and Jaleh Kilpatrick, from the Isle of Man; Derrick Nelson, formerly of the Isle of Man and a former colleague of Carolyn's; and my very good friend, the retired police inspector Angus Ailshie, also formerly of the Isle of Man, our host this afternoon."

Margaret sat down in the seat next to Carolyn, took a sip of water, and resumed. "What we want to do today is get some solid information from Carolyn and Derrick, which we will then pass along to the government attorney prosecuting Carolyn. In exchange for that information, she hopes to get a promise of leniency in her prosecution.

"Now, we understand that the government may want more than that; they will very likely be concerned about doing 'justice' in this particular case. I'm emphasizing the word 'justice' because Carolyn's crime was very, very bad; horrendous in fact. But it's important to understand and appreciate the difference between true justice and revenge; they are often used interchangeably but they are not the same."

Carolyn had been dreading this part of Margaret's presentation, and started tearing up, followed by sobbing. As the group waited for Carolyn to regain her composure, Margaret glanced and smiled at Jaleh, who set down her water glass and said, "Tom and I, and Angus as well, not to mention our dear friend Dimitri, are here to point out something that is very important to a proper understanding of justice. We have to remember something—not only the terrible thing that Carolyn did, the **criminal** thing she did, but also what the motivation was and what the result was. We all know what the motivation was; Carolyn has made that very clear—her overpowering fear of Bulent Aksoy, who had threatened to kill her if she did not repay her debt to him, a debt that she found impossible to repay once the government put a hold on her bank account pending its investigation into the illegal adoption scheme she and Derrick were operating. And also, it cannot be denied that Burt was a major player in Carolyn's motivation—he was a true coercer, and these two young men can attest to that, not only to Burt's manipulation of Carolyn but his manipulation of his late wife, Irene, Dani's mother and Dushan's stepmother.

"So let's look at the result of her crime. The result had two components. First, there was the incalculable pain she caused to Dushan and his parents. We cannot minimize that; Tom and I were witnesses to Dimitri and Marta's pain and suffering, which lasted for years!

"But then let's look at the result in its fullness; the 'result of the result,' as it were. Dushan has returned, a young, healthy, happy man. Not only that, but he has brought a new brother with him. These two young men grew up together, and are as close as two human beings can be. More than that, they have joined two families together. Dushan has two parents, two sisters, and loads of relatives living in Europe. Dani has uncountable family right here in England. What's more, the two of them have brought Thomas, Angus and myself into the family.

"Now, I don't know how much this matters to a government prosecutor, or a judge. But I certainly think it **might** make a difference in their thinking about justice, if Dani and Dushan talked to them about justice—true justice, not just retribution and punishment—justice tempered with mercy. The brothers are well acquainted with Carolyn, and they know that she is, or once was, a beloved member of the entire Sandor clan here in the British Isles. Carolyn is a blood relative of Dani. She is a niece of Dani's grandmother. Dushan is, for all intents and purposes, Dani's **brother**. And finally—I'm gonna shut up now!—they understand what happened to Carolyn, what pushed her to do this terrible thing, **who** pushed her into doing this."

When Jaleh sat back in her chair, Carolyn wasn't the only one with tears in her eyes—Dani and Dushan, Dimitri, and Charlotte were wiping their eyes as well. Charlotte raised her hand and asked to say a few words. "I just want to say that I can attest to the love between these two brothers. I was a frequent visitor at their home in southern California for a few years before my husband and I moved to New Jersey. The love Dani and Dushan felt for each other was genuine, powerful, impregnable! If my husband Gregory were still alive, he could attest to the malignant power Burt had over the family, and to how helpless these boys were to do anything about it. Gregory told me more than once that Burt exuded an evil 'vibe' that made Gregory so uncomfortable that he stopped coming with me to visit Irene and the boys."

Dani stood to pour himself another glass of orange juice, then sat back down and said, "You know, I could tell you many, many stories about the way my father manipulated people, including Carolyn, my mother, acquaintances, his co-workers and superiors, everyone. But we've already established that, and I see little point in going over that ground again. Nor is there any point in **my** telling you all about the pain Carolyn caused to Dushan. He's sitting right here beside me, and I think we should hear the story from him."

Dani stood as Dushan got up and walked over to him. They hugged and then sat back down. Dushan took a long look at Carolyn and then at his father. He sighed and said, "My dad and I have done a lot of thinking about this and I think we understand what has to be done. For my part, I gave up the idea of seeking revenge for what Carolyn did to me and my family a long time ago. Dani knows how my anger at her eventually dissipated as my focus—our focus— became centered on finding my father. And when we did that, we found my mother at the same time; and my two sisters as well! I can't really describe how that felt, to find my family again.

"So, all this stuff about what to do about Carolyn has very little to do with me emotionally. I understand why she did what she did; I don't necessarily forgive her for that. But I'm no longer angry or vengeful; neither is my dad. I don't think I ever truly hated her or wanted to do her harm.

"But I do think I have something to offer in achieving closure in Carolyn's case. Of course I agree that if she, and Mr. Nelson, can provide some information about Aksoy's operation that will probably gain her some advantage with the court. And if I ask the court to give her a break, that might also help her. But I believe the court will need more than those two things—it will need to understand how a little leniency toward her will work to the country's advantage. In other words, what can Carolyn do for her country, to paraphrase the late US president John Kennedy.

"Let's not overlook the fact that Carolyn had an excellent track record as a professional before she did what she did. She helped a lot of people, a lot of families. And she could do that again. She might even be able to rejoin her profession in different capacity. So, my input here is to suggest that Carolyn, Makelle, Thomas, Jaleh, Angus and Charlotte put their heads together and work on this idea, or something like it. Think about it—Makelle's a specialist in international criminal law who just spent a year in Liverpool teaching in that field. Thomas is lawyer intimately familiar with the legal landscape in the United Kingdom. Charlotte is related to half the Greek-British community in England and has lots of acquaintances in the shipping industry dating back to when she and Greg were still working in Liverpool. Jaleh has been working with refugees from all over Europe and the Middle East for 30 years. Carolyn, of course, was a skilled and dedicated social worker who helped settle refugees. Angus is intimately familiar with the law enforcement communities and their programs all over the UK." Dushan looked over at Dani and said, "Okay; I'm done. Over and out."

Dani smiled and said, "You're not quite done yet. You forgot a very important person, someone who might work with Carolyn in the refugee problem in the UK."

Dushan slapped his forehead and said, "You're right, Cap'n Dante. My great grandmother Shimza's 'setting up shop' here in Liverpool and will hopefully be working with a social service agency here dedicated to helping the Rom refugees get their new lives together."

Angus rose from the couch, stretched and said, "I think we might want to take a little break and get some sun in the backyard, before the sun disappears. My teapot is on the simmer. I'll make us some tea and join you in a few minutes." As people were getting up, Carolyn said, "Wait just a second. I have to tell everyone, especially Dushan, that I have some information on Bulent Aksoy, lots of good information. But I think we'll feel better hearing about him in the sunshine." Derrick nodded and said, "I also have some information. Somehow, with all these friends surrounding us, I no longer feel like I have to hide from Aksoy. We're going to find him and put him away for a long time."

CHAPTER ELEVEN:
THE ISLE OF MAN
July 2014

When Marta put down the phone, she rubbed her eyes as if coming out of a dream. She and the girls had just arrived at their youth hostel in Douglas after a long flight from Ljubljana, when the desk clerk called the room to say there was a phone message. The message was from Nonna, asking Marta to call her upon their arrival. *I can't understand why grandma doesn't get a cell phone. It would sure be a lot more convenient if she did.* Marta called her back as soon as they had unpacked. Nonna told her that the girls' admission to St. Ninian's was "likely" a done deal. They were to take a taxi to meet with the headmaster the next morning at 10 a.m. and discuss the girls' admission!

For the rest of that afternoon, Marta and her daughters did a little sightseeing. That evening they had a delicious seafood dinner at a restaurant in the harbor. They were back in the hostel by 9 p.m., in time for an hour's worth of visiting with some of the other guests—mostly young people touring the island. When they went to bed at the mandatory 10 p.m. lights-out, they fell asleep almost instantly.

The next morning, as they sat in the headmaster's office listening to his plans for them that morning, Marta and the girls realized that not only was the girls' admission to St. Ninian's "likely," it was a fait accompli. *It would seem my grandmother's persuasive powers are even stronger in her old age,* was the thought Marta was rolling around in her mind. She looked over at Aisha and her sister Shimza, who were eagerly perusing the glossy promotional materials the headmaster, Dr. Michael Brady, had handed them. The twins were 14 years old, and wanted to impress upon Dr. Brady that they were merely considering their options for their freshman year of high school, notwithstanding that they were eagerly anticipating their move to Douglas and St. Ninian's.

Brady smiled and said, "Now, the first thing I've scheduled for you is a meeting with several faculty members, who will show you some of the departmental offices and classrooms. Professor Colin Edmonds, a Seattle guy who 'went native' after his first year here as a brand-new computer science teacher in 1978, will show you around a bit before handing you over to Professor Ron Mallinder, our resident 'mad scientist' in the Physics Department, formerly of Robert College of Istanbul. He's known as 'Mad Mallinder' to some students, but don't tell him I said that.

"After that, you'll be our guests for lunch in the faculty cafeteria, where you'll meet Professor Suna Göksel, Professor Mallinder's Turkish wife. She will show you around the Maths Department classrooms, where she teaches, and introduce you to some of the professors on the faculty. Next, you'll get a tour of the dorms, gymnasium, and sports field."

Marta smiled and spoke up. "Thank you Dr. Brady, but I don't think the girls will be living in the dorms. We'll be looking around at houses and hope to purchase one within the next few weeks."

Ayesha, with a look of polite resolution on her face, said, "Mom, Shimza and I think we'd prefer living in the dorms. That way, we can get into the school community more quickly."

Dr. Brady looked at Marta as she appeared to be trying to decide how to respond to her daughter's announcement. He said, "Whatever you decide is fine, I'm sure. No need to make that decision just yet. You just let me know when you know."

By 4 o'clock, the sisters and their mom were exhausted and over the top with excitement. They walked down the hill to the main road leading to Douglas proper and climbed into a half-empty "share taxi" servicing the local shopping district. The car became more and more crowded as additional passengers flagged down and hopped into the car. Nevertheless, Marta and the twins enjoyed the scenic ride along the shore of the Irish Sea.

That evening they had dinner with Nonna, who had taken the ferry over from Liverpool a few days before and had met with Dr. Brady. She told them she called Dr. Brady after they left the campus. "He seemed very impressed with your school records, and is pleased that he can offer to admit the girls. They'll be among the first small group of students from the former Yugoslavia."

After Nonna left to return to Liverpool, the girls decided they wanted to accept Dr. Brady's offer of admission, and they let Marta know in no uncertain terms. First thing after dinner, Marta called the school and left a message on Dr. Brady's voicemail telling him they had decided. They would return two weeks before the fall semester began to get settled and ready for their intensive class in the Manx language, required of all foreign students. After that seven-day week of intensive language class, the academic semester would begin. Their classes would be taught in English except for whatever foreign language elective they decided on; none of their classes would be in Manx, unless they wanted to continue with Manx as their foreign language. Shimza told her mom she would like to continue with Manx and become fluent. Aisha was not so sure; she thought perhaps she would concentrate on French.

CHAPTER TWELVE:
BIG CHANGES IN THE SAVA FAMILY

Dushan and Dimitri had been back home from England for over a week when Marta and the twins returned to Ljubljana from their whirlwind three-day trip to Douglas. The men were so brimming over with excitement in the telling of their "highly successful" stay in Liverpool that they were surprised when it became obvious that Marta and the twins were **more** excited about their **own** trip—to the Isle of Man.

"Dad, Dushan," Shimza said, "you just cannot believe how beautiful St. Ninian's is! And Douglas! My God, it's amazing! We're gonna go to school there. Mom already told the headmaster."

Dimitri put down his coffee cup, picked up the St. Ninian's welcome packet, and thumbed through the pages. He was visibly impressed at the beautiful campus displayed in the brochure.

"Well, Dushan, should we allow these girls to head off across the Irish Sea?" He smiled and said to Marta, "I take it you have given this careful consideration? Is the city safe? Can we afford it?"

"Yes to all three questions, my dear. The city is very safe, safer than most European cities. And the school has offered the girls a very generous scholarship. We'll just have to pay for their room and board in the dorm. So, it won't cost us much more than the cost of feeding these two at home."

After Shimza and Aisha spent the next 15 minutes taking turns describing in minute detail all the things they had seen on and off campus, Shimza dug a different brochure out of her backpack. Handing it to Dushan, she said, "Take a look at University College Isle of Man. Nonna gave it to us the evening before we left for home. She said you should check it out. They have a great International Relations department, and Nonna says she can arrange for an interview for you with the department chair. Also, Dr. Brady told us that University College is connected to a university in the UK proper. Wouldn't it be cool if you could go there while we're at St. Ninian's?"

Dushan thumbed through the brochure and did a double take as he opened it up to a two-page photo of the college campus. "Wow, these are very beautiful buildings," pointing to a couple of magnificent edifices from the late 19th century.

"You need to come with us, Dushan. You've got to see Douglas. You'll love it!"

Glancing at his parents, Dushan said, "Well, I don't have anything else going at the moment, especially don't have any other college plans cooking. What do you say, mom and dad, should I check it out? I'm pretty rich, you know, after Dani and I inherited his old man's estate in California and Dani's grandmother gifted us with the remains of the Sandor Family Trust."

Dimitri smiled and said, "Sure, it can't hurt to at least check it out. Maybe your mom's grandma can pull some strings, like she obviously did with Dr. Brady."

Marta laughed, "I'm not kidding, guys, you should have seen how smooth the whole interview went with Dr. Brady. And I get the feeling Nonna had a lot to do with that. That being the case, I wouldn't be surprised if she couldn't pull another rabbit out of the hat with University College."

Dimitri said, "Now, do you three busy world travellers have time to listen to what Dushan accomplished in Liverpool? Talk about miracles!"

Marta looked at Dushan with a concerned expression and said, "I can't imagine how difficult that must have been, my dear. What was she like?"

"I had her and everyone else in tears when I was done working my magic on her." Laughter filled the room, and Dushan continued. "Actually, I just pointed out that Carolyn had a lot to gain from cooperating with the authorities in tracking down this creep that was running the trafficking network in Europe. She and her former partner in crime, Derrick Nelson, said they thought they knew how to find him, and Angus—you remember him, Mom, the retired cop from Isle of Man—said he could set up some sort of sting to finally take him off the streets."

Marta asked, "And Carolyn? When's her next court date and what's the likelihood the court will give her a break?"

"She's due in court for a status hearing in two weeks. By then she may have some information on the search for Bulent Aksoy. Makelle Ringhiera—the law professor from San Francisco who's some kind of nephew of Danilo's grandmother—has requested leave to address the court to fill the judge in on the status of the search. Makelle thinks the court will be very inclined to sentence Carolyn to probation or a short jail term **if**, and that's a very big if, she helps the police shut Aksoy down."

Aisha asked, "Was Danilo there when you guys had the meeting with Carolyn? What are his plans?"

"Yes, he was there for moral support. And afterwards he hung out with me and dad and everyone. He took us out to this nightclub to hear some so-called 'gypsy jazz.' You won't believe this but when Dani introduced us to a woman in the band, Jaelle Ringhiera, Makelle told her, and us, that she's his daughter, for God's sake! Apparently he had a fling with a fellow student back in his college days in California, and this young woman is the fruit of that relationship. What a story! Jaelle laughed and told Makelle that her mom had already told her about him, and also told her that Makelle was in town teaching at the university.

"But the good news about Dani is that he just enrolled as a freshman at Liverpool University. He's living in a cottage in his grandmother's backyard in town. The dude's got it made. Plus, he's already working on a family reunion plan for all of us to get together somewhere in December or January. When I told him that our family would be relocating to the Isle of Man, he said maybe he'd talk his buddy Claude into joining us all there or in Liverpool; or maybe Ireland."

Shimza clapped her hands and said, "See! This will be perfect. You come with us to Douglas and apply to University College. Danilo and Claude come over during winter break and we can all do some serious sightseeing!"

CHAPTER THIRTEEN:
AN UNEXPECTED REUNION

In the midst of all the excitement over Dushan's and the girls' upcoming late-August school enrollments in Douglas and Dani's in Liverpool, and the more immediate trip in a week or so to Douglas to look at real estate, Marta got a phone call from Milan Vukadin, her friend from back when he was a Red Cross driver and she was a public health nurse in Sarajevo. The two of them had escaped the Serbian assault on Sarajevo in 1992, and Marta began working as a nurse in Belgrade. A few years after that, after marrying Dimitri and giving birth to Dushan, Marta was kidnapped by rogue elements of the Serbian army and forced to work as a nurse in an army camp in Novi Pazar under Goran Bolat, her husband's former employee who had become an officer in the Serbian army. It was Milan who, along with his old high school friend Jovan Durkovic, by then a draftee in the Serbian army, facilitated Marta's escape. Milan had learned of Marta's indentured servitude when he ran into Jovan in Belgrade. Milan and Jovan not only freed Marta, but also her friend Seifullah Hamid, a prisoner at the camp who had been forced to serve the army brass as an interpreter and servant.

Now Milan was telling her that he was in Ljubljana for a few days and was hoping to be able to hook up with her and Dimitri and the family. Milan added, "Seif says he can take time off from his job at the Ljubljana mosque and join us. My job at the Red Cross center in Trieste is slowing down a bit, so I thought maybe we could do some sightseeing in your area. Lake Bled?"

"Sure sounds good to me. I haven't been there since I was a teenager. But when you say you want to visit our family, I'm afraid you'll have to be satisfied with just me. Dimitri, Dushan and the twins are visiting Dimitri's aunt in Belgrade before we all head up to the Isle of Man."

"Isle of Man! Doing what?"

"You remember when I wrote to tell you the good news that Dushan found us after all those years living with the California family that had basically stolen him from Dimitri? He not only found us, but he introduced us to his "stepbrother," Danilo, who he had grown up with. Well, to make a long story short, our whole family has decided to relocate to the Isle of Man so the girls and Dushan could go to school there and Dushan could stay close to Danilo, who will go to college across the water in Liverpool."

"Fantastic! Give them my congratulations. I was so looking forward to finally seeing them, but I guess it'll have to wait. So, what do you say, are you ready to play tour guide?"

Marta chuckled and said, "Sure; and I'll let Jovan Durkovic know that you're in town. Do you two keep in touch?"

"Sure do; he even visited me a while back. He already knows about my plan, and is trying to free up some time. He says he gets to see you on a fairly regular basis."

"That's right. He's an auditor with the World Health Organization's 'European Healthy Cities Network' here in Ljubljana. My clinic, the Ljubljana Community Health Center, is the largest health center in Slovenia, and we have a good working relationship with Jovan's office. But I'll really miss him once we relocate to the Isle of Man."

"I sure hope he can join us."

*   *   *

When Milan stepped off the train at the Ljubljana station, he was met by Marta, Jovan and Seif. Marta said, "How was the trip? I'm surprised your train arrived right on time. That's probably a first!"

Milan gave her a big hug. "The trip was great. It's been a long time, Marta. Has it really been almost 12 years?"

"I think so. Seems like yesterday, though. Look at you—still the same studly guy who smuggled me out of the Novi Pazar army camp."

Milan placed his hand on Jovan's shoulder and said, "It was all this genius's doing. He figured it all out. And Seif, how are you doing my brother?"

A big smile on his face, Seif said, "Just fine. Better than fine.

Moving up in the Muslim community; I am now the chief operating officer at the mosque. Got a family—wife and two daughters. Things couldn't be better."

Milan turned to Jovan and said, "So, Mr. Big Shot. It's good to see you again. When was it you came to visit me in Trieste? Five, six years ago?"

"Eight; you're losing track of time, my friend."

Marta said, "Okay, guys, let's hop in my van and hit the road. I want us to get to the lake before dark. Maybe we can do a little swimming if the water's not too cold."

*   *   *

Marta pulled up and parked at a drop-dead gorgeous hotel practically right on the lake. "Here we are, boys, our home for the next couple of days—the Hotel Jelovica Bled."

The friends wasted no time checking in, stowing their bags, and walking to the lake shore, bathing suits in hand. When they got to hotel's little expanse of private beach, Marta looked out at the whitecaps rolling across the lake's surface and said, "Hmm, I don't know if swimming is such a good idea after all. This breeze will make for a chilly experience." Looking down the shore, she pointed to a boat rental facility a couple of hundred yards away. "What do you say we rent a boat? We can pay a visit to Bled Island and walk around the beautiful former church that's now a museum."

Everyone thought this would be a great alternative to swimming in a chilly lake. The drive took a few minutes. They parked in the customer lot at the boat rental shed and perused the boats. Milan pointed out a rather grandiose looking boat and said, "That's for me, a dragon boat! Looks like it can fit us all." There were no disagreements, so they all boarded and the muscular boatman shoved away from the dock with powerful oar strokes.

One of the other boatmen watched the departing group with particular interest; incredulity, in fact. He **knew** every one of them. "How long it's been, and I still remember their faces," Goran Bolat muttered to himself as he finished tying up his own boat to the pier.

It had been almost 18 years since Goran's court-martial, but the humiliation and hurt from the experience still poisoned his dreams. Busted in rank from major in the Yugoslavian National Army, and then discharged dishonorably with forfeiture of back pay, Goran found himself penniless and unemployable in war-torn Yugoslavia. Not even his family in Belgrade could help him out. But a cousin in Slovenia came to his rescue.

"Lake Bled, where the hell is that?" Goran shouted into the pay phone as he waited for a bus in Belgrade. He tried to mask his impatience and skepticism as curiosity, but he could tell his cousin was getting a little annoyed.

"Slovenia, an hour out of Ljubljana by bus. Look, it's a beautiful place and the job isn't too hard, if you don't mind a fair amount of physical exertion. You'd work in one of the boathouses—some rowing tourists around the lake, some maintenance on the boats and equipment, and a furnished room next to a boathouse you can stay in for free. And who knows, maybe you'll meet a nice matronly German tourist, get married and live happily ever after in Munich or someplace."

After spending the summer months living homeless on the streets of Belgrade, his relocation to Lake Bled in October probably saved him from freezing to death during the approaching winter. In the years since, Goran grew to love the physical beauty of the lake and the little villages and towns around the lake and in the region. Ljubljana was also a source of balm to him as well, especially when he recalled the urban chaos of Belgrade.

But not a single day since then did Goran let go of his anger and determination to get back at Marta Cecelja and the two miscreants who tricked him into allowing her "transfer" out of his custody. Corporal Jovan Durkovic and that phony Red Cross guy, Milan something, showed Goran a document signed by a Colonel "ordering" Marta's transfer. To top it off, Marta prevailed on Goran to allow that Muslim Turk, "Seif" something, to go with them. Goran never could figure out how that group managed to talk him into the "transfer." *Marta must have been some sort of witch*, he said to himself more than once. He could recall the mental push from Marta that persuaded him to approve the transfer—it was like a feeling just came over him, a feeling that approving the transfer would give him peace; refusing the transfer would cause stress. *Why didn't I realize what she was doing?*

Looking back on it, he realized he should never have called the brass in Belgrade to let them know of Marta's transfer. When he read the order to the colonel whose signature appeared on the order, the colonel went ballistic and accused Goran of carelessness in accepting a document without a confirmation. A few hours after that phone call, one of Goran's superiors in the camp approached him, informed him of the "very serious charge of citizen abduction," and put him under arrest. Goran was astounded at the irony in the situation. His colonel was angry at Goran for having allowed the escape of a much-needed nurse, but subsequently had him arrested on a different charge. Goran reminded the arresting officer that what he did was what many did in his position when they were short of medical or logistical personnel. It didn't work, even when he added that his "arrest" of Marta was based on her notoriety as a "troublemaker" who was creating instability in Belgrade with her incessant public commentary and demonstrations criticizing the government and army.

By all accounts, Goran's punishment could have been worse than it was. After all, in those desperate and lawless times during the breakup of Yugoslavia, soldiers were shot for any number of derelictions of duty. He recalled the chilling conclusion of the closing argument of the colonel acting as the prosecutor at the court-martial trial. "Our country cannot allow such criminality on the part of our military, especially our officers. It seems clear that Major Bolat approved the abduction of this nurse *because he was attracted to her!*"

The prosecutor was an extreme right-wing fellow Serb who nonetheless was out for Goran's blood. Goran and his defense counsel, a somewhat more liberal Slovenian officer from Ljubljana, were shocked by the irony in the prosecution's case against Goran. On the one hand, there was no doubt that Goran had been holding Marta against her will and forcing her to work as a nurse in the army's encampment in Novi Pazar. But the irony was that she was far from the only such abductee forced to work for the army. It was a common practice in those days, especially when the abductee's skills matched the army unit's needs in a particular location. But the military judge would not allow that defense to be raised in the case. That "common practice" was not something that the military wanted to be publicized.

So, a conviction was foreordained. It was only Goran's "connections" that saved him from a lengthy prison term, or even the firing squad. His uncle was an army careerist who had risen to two-star general and served on the Croatian front. Thanks to his plea for leniency, Goran dodged a bullet (figuratively or literally, he shuddered to think) and avoided a prison term.

Notwithstanding his uncle's influence on the court-martial judge, that influence had zero effect on the army brass's ability to make sure Goran would never work again in Belgrade or anywhere else in Serbia. It was Goran's uncle's son in Ljubljana who saved Goran's bacon. Milosz was not only a cousin but a childhood friend who had grown up in Belgrade and only recently moved to Ljubljana.

Even so, Milosz's generosity in scoring a job for Goran did little or nothing to heal the wound he felt since his court-martial. Nor did the physical beauty of Lake Bled, its healthful air, and the modest degree of responsibility he had recently achieved with his promotion to boat master, take away from the searing hatred he felt for Marta. In his mind she was a witch for sure. Goran would bide his time. He felt sure he would meet her again. His dreams of her confirmed that certainty.

His thirst for vengeance was intensified by the physical attraction to her he once felt. That and his tangled emotions arising from the fact that he had in effect stolen her away from his former friend and civilian employer, Dimitri Sava, her husband, not to mention taking her away from their child. During the two or three years Goran had "employed" Marta to work as an indentured nurse in his army camp in Novi Pazar, Goran had grown to like her more and more, never mind the fact that he had taken her away from her husband and child.

He stepped out onto the ground, lit a cigarette and considered what his next steps would be. His thoughts popped up in random order—*What am I doing here? Shall I remain a boat monkey the rest of my days? Will I ever have a chance to see these criminals again? No; they'll be gone forever if I don't do something! I mustn't let this opportunity slip through my fingers. My life is about to change.*

All the pieces of his vision came together. He walked quickly to his cabin next to the boathouse, threw some clothes and important papers into a suitcase, and retrieved his prized service pistol from its hiding place in the closet. *They may have taken my honor from me, but they never managed to find this!* Loading and shoving the pistol into his waistband, he walked out to the employee parking area, threw the suitcase into a company van and locked it. Then he walked over to the nearest dragon boat and said to the other oarsmen, "I'm heading over to the island to relieve Karl. When I saw him leave with that foursome I realized I knew a couple of them. I'm gonna go over and surprise them. It's close to quitting time, so don't send over any more tourists. Except for that group, the island is deserted anyway."

When Goran pulled up and docked the boat at the island, he saw that Karl's boat was docked at the other pier about 50 yards to Goran's left; it was the only boat left on the island. Karl hadn't seen Goran yet; he was sitting on the front of the boat, his back to Goran, having a smoke. Goran stood for a moment to collect his thoughts. His thoughts began a little debate in his mind: *Are you sure you wanna do this? Okay, but make sure Karl leaves without suspecting anything. What about that former Army guy, Jovan? Will he try to be a tough guy and fight me? The others are all pussies, I have no doubt; however, this Jovan could be trouble. But I can't just shoot him; the noise would be heard all around the lake. We'll play it by ear; maybe he's not in the mood to get hurt.*

Goran walked up noisily to Karl and said, "Karl my friend. Guess what? When I saw you leave with that group, I realized I knew a couple of them. I'm gonna play a little surprise on them. I'll meet them in the church museum; you can head on back. I've told the others to lock things up and go home for the day. Kind of slow, anyway and it's getting dark."

Goran watched Karl shove off and, when Karl was halfway back across the lake, Goran retrieved a coil of rope from his boat and started walking up to the former church. When he reached the entrance, he heard voices coming from inside the ornate main room. He ducked into an alcove directly across from one of the semi-private rooms set up for pilgrims wishing to pray to Saint Mary. His plan was to wait for the group to begin walking back toward the entrance to the main sanctuary, and accost them as they reached his location. From there, he would force them at gunpoint into the small room. After that, he thought he would order Marta to tie the others up. He knew the lake administrator's cabin cruiser was docked at the other side of the island. He would herd his sheep to the boat and motor back to the lakeshore. *We're going to go on a little vacation, all of us,* he thought as he prepared himself for what was to come.

As it turned out, Goran didn't have to force them to enter the prayer room after all; Marta walked right in and the others followed.

This will be easier than I hoped, Goran thought.

He stepped into the room, pistol in hand, deliberately making enough noise to get their attention. The group turned around almost in unison, and found themselves facing a man aiming a gun at them and grinning in a most unsettling way.

Marta screamed, "Oh my God, I can't believe it. **YOU!**" Without thinking, she mentally pushed a bolt of pure aggression at Goran. He flinched, but his grin only grew bigger. "Save your strength, bitch. We're going on a trip. But first, do me a favor. Everyone on the floor, face down, facing the wall; **NOW!**" Laying his coil of rope on the ground, he knelt and cut four three-foot lengths of rope. Standing up again, he shouted, "Now, put your hands together behind you with wrists together! **Do it!**" He fired a round into the wall to his right to let them know he wasn't playing games. When the group complied, Goran said to Marta, "Get up and tie their hands, tight! Anyone moves, they get shot."

After Goran checked the tightness of Marta's work, he took the last piece of cut rope and tied Marta's hands himself.

At this point, Jovan spoke up. "Listen, Major Bolat, sir. This whole thing was my fault. I'm the one who talked you into releasing Marta and Séif. I falsified that order from your superior. Marta and Seif, as well as Milan, had no idea the order was false. If you want to punish someone, punish me. The others are completely innocent. They thought the whole thing was above board."

Goran walked over to Jovan and kicked him in the ribs. "That's very sweet and loyal of you, Corporal. But I'm afraid I don't believe you. However, I will commend your loyalty when we get to our destination and I speak with the officer in charge."

Stepping out of the little prayer room into the main room, Goran looked through the front door at the darkening sky. He walked back and announced to the hostages, "We're gonna wait til it's completely dark before we move. So, get comfy."

It was over an hour before Goran felt it was safe to take the group out of the building and make their way to the boss's cabin cruiser at the service dock. After marching the group onto the boat, he ordered them to lie face down on the floor. He started the engine and motored over to the shore. The rental area was deserted at that hour, and Goran was pretty sure he hadn't been noticed. Unlocking the lake's panel van parked in the lot, he ordered everyone into the van.

He decided he would take his captives across the Slovenia-Croatia border, through Croatia to the Serbian border post just beyond Tovarnik, a six-hour trip. He would turn Jovan in as a Serb deserter who arranged the "theft" of Goran's prisoners of war, Seif and Marta, with the assistance of Milan. His hope was to have his court-martial overturned and be returned to the Army reserves.

After the captives were in the company van he told Marta she would drive, and ordered the others to lie on the bare floor of the van. Marta stepped up to the driver's seat, Goran untied her hands, gave her instructions, and they were on their way.

*   *   *

It was after 10 o'clock when Karl Strauss realized he had left his cell phone in the glove box of the lake's panel van. He had been planning on calling his daughter in Amsterdam to wish her happy birthday, so he decided to drive back to the lake to retrieve the phone. "She's no doubt at a party somewhere; I'm sure my call won't wake her up," he muttered as he started up his car and began driving.

He was shocked to see the panel van was missing from the employee parking lot. What was also strange was that there was a car still parked in the public lot, long after lake visitors were required to leave the area. *What was it Goran said? He knew the group on the island?* Karl walked along the shore to the maintenance shed to see if the dragon boat had been returned, as Goran said he would do. Nothing. Not only that, but the boss's cabin cruiser was moored in the slot where the dragon boat should have been.

Karl drove back home, woke up his computer, and opened the program that would allow him to track his cell phone, which he was sure he had not turned off. The locator indicated its current location was just before Slovenia's border with Croatia, approximately 40 miles from Zagreb. *Shit, that's more than two hours from here. What the hell's he doing with the panel van? And where are those tourists? Are they with him? What's going on?*

In less than an hour, two Slovenian highway patrol officers were on their way to Zagreb, after having notified the Slovenian and Croatian border police of the presumed theft of the company panel van and possible kidnapping of four people. The apparently abandoned SUV at Lake Bled had been determined to belong to

Marta Cecelja and Dimitri Sava of Ljubljana. The local police called Dimitri's cell phone and learned the identities of Marta and the other three passengers—Jovan Durkovic, Milan Vukadin and Seifullah Hamid. After the call, Dimitri hopped into his Land Rover and headed for Serbia's border with Croatia, trying to rendezvous with the Slovenian highway patrol who left half an hour earlier.

While the police were searching Marta's car, Karl took a look around inside Goran's cabin. In the drawer of the nightstand next to the bed, Karl saw a notebook. He thumbed through it, and saw it was a journal or diary. There were frequent references to Goran's hope to reverse his court-martial and get his army commission back. "Impossible," Karl muttered as he read Goran's crazy idea. Page after page, Goran poured out his anger at "Marta" and the "lowlifes" who helped her escape from "lawful custody" under Goran's command.

Karl immediately informed the police that Goran's ultimate destination was probably Belgrade, and handed over Goran's journal. *So, it would appear that my supervisor has put his insane plan into motion!*

CHAPTER FOURTEEN:
TROUBLE AT THE BORDER

It was at least an hour before anyone spoke—anyone except Goran, who occasionally barked directions to the driver, Marta, and repeated his orders to the others to stay on the floor of the van. After Marta had been driving on the highway for a while, she turned to Goran as he sat in the front passenger seat cradling his pistol in his lap. "So, Goran, would you mind telling me where we're going, and why?" She had a strong feeling they were headed for the Serbian border, but couldn't discern Goran's plans for them after that.

"You're a pretty smart lady. I think you've got it figured out already."

"What do you hope to gain by taking us all to Belgrade or wherever?"

"Very good. You're a mind reader. You tell me what you think I'm planning."

"Well, give me a clue. Does it have anything to do with our having escaped your lovely little slave camp?"

Jovan jumped into the conversation. "I think that's exactly what's going on, Marta. I'm guessing he got in trouble for releasing you and Seif. Am I close, Major?"

Goran turned and leveled his pistol at Jovan. "Got in trouble, you say? How about ruined my life. **YOU** ruined my life. I lost my career, almost faced a firing squad. All because of you, Mr. Durkovic!"

Marta jumped back into the conversation. "If you don't mind, Goran, I'd like us to revisit those days, just for a few minutes. Maybe you can explain to me why you thought you had the right to take me from my child and husband and enslave me for those years. Do you actually think that was legal, let alone ethical, what you did?"

Goran practically choked with his anger. "You were a well-known thorn in the side of the government in Belgrade. Constantly harping on imagined civil rights abuses; letters to the editor, rants on call-in talk shows; little speeches at community meetings. Everyone in the government wanted you gone. I just did my duty and took you away. Problem solved. Anything else you want to know?"

"And now you think you're going to turn us all in as if we were escaped convicts? How deluded you must be if you think that."

"Just shut up and drive. We'll see who's the deluded one when we reach the Serbian border." Goran stopped talking and kept his gun trained on the three men in the back. Marta sighed and refocused her attention on the road. She kept her speed down not only because it was dark and the road was in poor shape, but mostly in the hope that the police or someone might be able to follow them.

*   *   *

Karl checked on the location of his cell phone for the third time and texted the Slovenian highway patrol officers who were pursuing the vehicle. By this time, Goran's van was well inside Croatia, getting close to Tovarnik on the Serbian border. The Slovenes, in turn, notified the Croatian national police and Serbian border police of the approaching vehicle.

It was a little after dawn when Goran and company drew near the Serbian border. "Shit; what the hell!" Goran was staring with disbelief at the immense crowd of people on foot and in cars amassed on and around the road on the Serbian side. Dozens of Croatian police were blocking the crowd's access to the Croatian side of the border. Marta slowed the van and came to a stop about 100 yards before the border.

"Now what, genius?" She was trying not to anger Goran, but it was hard to keep from smiling or, worse yet, chuckling. "There's no way they're gonna allow us to go across the border through that crowd. There must be a thousand people, probably those Middle Eastern migrants we've been reading about. Look, the agents are turning some vehicles around."

"Just keep going as long as you can. We'll be at the border station in a few minutes. They're letting some commercial vehicles through. Maybe they'll let ours through."

When they got a little closer to the border, Marta could see a

Serbian border officer scanning the traffic. When he saw the van he stared closely, then turned around and spoke to a man in a soldier's uniform. Turning back, the border officer motioned the van to move into the left lane and proceed past the cars ahead of them. Goran broke into a big smile and said, "Yes! We made it. We'll be past this crowd in no time!"

Marta drove the van across the border and followed the border officer's hand signal to a small building a few yards to the left of the highway. Goran spoke as Marta pulled up in front of the building. "I don't understand. Maybe they've got new border controls now with all this migration crisis going on."

Marta parked, opened the driver's door and stepped out, avoiding Goran's attempt to grab her and stop her. The Serbian soldier was walking toward the passenger side of the van. Goran tucked his gun in his waistband under his shirt and stepped out. "Officer, I've got some former prisoners of war for you. It's taken a long time, but I finally captured them." Goran started to slide open the van's side door, but the soldier spun him around and slammed him up against it. "Welcome home, Major Bolat. We've been awaiting your arrival. And your so-called prisoners' arrival."

Goran punched the soldier with his left fist, reached into his waistband with his right hand and pulled out the gun. He managed to fire one round, but missed. He missed because at the moment he fired, the van's side door slid the rest of the way open and knocked Goran to the right. Seif tumbled out onto the ground, hands still tied behind his back. The soldier grabbed the gun from Goran and kicked him to the ground.

Seif scrambled to his feet and Marta began untying his hands. Jovan and Milan climbed out of the van and Seif and Marta untied their hands. Everyone turned back to watch Goran being handcuffed. The soldier handed Goran over to another soldier, who led him to a vehicle that looked like a HumVee and shoved him inside. At that moment, the two Slovenian highway patrol officers who had followed the van all the way from Ljubljana pulled up and got out of their patrol car. The driver said to Marta, "We followed you from the Slovenian border, but you were too far ahead for us to catch up."

"What do you mean? How did you know where we were headed?"

The other officer reached into the passenger side of the van and opened the glove compartment. He reached in and removed a cell phone. "This phone led us here. It belongs to Mr. Karl Strauss, a Lake Bled employee. When he discovered it missing, he tracked it on his computer and alerted us."

Marta reached for the phone. "Mind if I call my husband on that phone? And my daughters and son?"

The officer handed Karl's phone to her and stepped away to see how the other captives were doing. "Well," he said to the Serbian soldier interviewing them, "what have you learned about this incident? Who is this creep who kidnapped these folks?"

The soldier looked up and scratched his head. "All we know so far is that the guy is an embittered ex-soldier who had some kind of dispute with these three."

Milan spoke up when the soldier paused. "We're friends of theirs and the woman's husband, Dimitri Sava. We all lived in Serbia in those days. Goran Bolat, the guy you've arrested, used to work for Dimitri back before joining the Yugoslavian army at the outset of the civil war. He was obsessed with Marta and ordered her abduction. He forced her to work as a nurse in one of the army's forward positions up north. When I learned she had been taken, I enlisted the aid of my old friend here," indicating Jovan, "and we convinced the major to allow Marta and her medical assistant, Seif right here, to help the Red Cross in a nearby hospital." As Milan spoke, Seif and Jovan were watching him nervously, hoping he wouldn't mention that Jovan was in the army at the time. *Not to worry*, Milan signaled to them with a wink.

The soldier smiled and said, "Okay. I've got to help out with booking our prisoner. I'll let my Slovenian colleagues escort you home if you like."

"That won't be necessary, officer." Marta walked up and handed back the cell phone. "My husband Dimitri is on his way, and Karl Strauss, the Lake Bled employee in charge of this van, is also on his way with his supervisor. They should be here in less than an hour. We'll just wait for them if you don't mind. Karl will retrieve the van when you're done processing it, and my husband will drive the rest of us home in our SUV."

CHAPTER FIFTEEN:
PARTY ON THE ISLE

Marta and the girls returned to Douglas on Friday, August 22, two weeks after Marta's escape from Goran. Marta honestly wondered whether she shouldn't just stay in bed for a few days before launching back into real life. But real life demanded she jump back in the game. Dimitri and Dushan had returned a few days earlier to finalize the family's purchase of a small home on a hill above the Douglas harbor. It was now two weeks before classes would start at St. Ninian's and almost a month before Dushan's classes would begin at University College. Marta said, "Well, folks, we have our work cut out for us. We've got a house to furnish, a car and rental van to unload, bicycles, school books and uniforms to buy, and—for your father and me—new jobs to prepare for. Let's get busy!"

Dushan spent the first day helping to unload the rental van and unpack boxes. The following day he devoted to exploring Douglas and University College. Day three was spent getting registered in the classes he hoped to take.

The process of signing up for classes was pretty easy—he did it all online from his laptop. He was fortunate to get spots in four of his first choices—World History, Sociology, Archeology and International Legal Systems. Each of the class listings provided the name of the professor in charge, sometimes accompanied by links for further information. The person who taught International Legal Systems was a visiting law professor from San Francisco—Bernard Siegal of Golden Gate University. *Hmm, I wonder if he knows Makelle. Probably does.* But he couldn't get into the French class he was planning on. He was required to take either a foreign language— French being the only one offered—or the native celtic language, Manx. Not having a choice, he signed up for Manx. *I wonder if*

Liverpool U. offers Manx. I'm gonna suggest Dani take it.

With over three weeks to kill, and a house full of excited family members, he invited Dani and Dani's grandmother Margaret to come across the water from Liverpool and pay the Sava family a visit. After they had been there for two days, Dushan invited his great grandmother Shimza to join the party. She had only recently moved from Istanbul to the Picton district of Liverpool to work with the Rom community there and was extremely busy. But she said she could spare a Friday-through-Monday visit with them. Dushan told her to call him when she arrived at the ferry terminal and he would pick her up.

During their phone conversation he asked her how she liked her new home. She said, "I love Liverpool, even though it's not as exotic as Istanbul. My apartment is in a beautiful neighborhood and walking distance from my new job!"

First thing Friday morning, Nonna caught the ferry. She didn't have to wait at all after the Steam Packet pulled into the Douglas ferry terminal; Dushan was waiting for her. On the way to the new house from the ferry terminal, Dushan told Nonna about the dreams and daydreams he had about the way Nonna's Istanbul apartment had looked. "I kept seeing an old, ramshackle apartment, with a view of the water, a couple of cats sleeping in the window, and books lying all over the place in piles. I wish I'd been able to visit you down there."

"Your dreams were not far off, except that before moving to that apartment you dreamt about, which was barely 50 years old, I lived in a 19th century Ottoman 'yalı' in the old part of Istanbul. It was basically a two-story duplex with a family living on the bottom floor and me on the top floor. The stairs were getting to be too much for me, so I moved. The apartment was close to the Grand Bazaar and I walked there almost every day. When you visit me in Picton, I'll show you some of the stuff I acquired in Istanbul over the years."

There wasn't one minute of social awkwardness. Even though Dushan hadn't had the bounty of growing up with his great grandmother, it felt like he had known her all his life. As he pulled into the driveway of their new house, he thought, *I'm gonna enjoy hangin' out with Nonna. This is great.*

When they walked into the foyer of the house, the first person to see them was Marta, who was unpacking a box of porcelean figurines

Dimitri had inherited from a great aunt in Belgrade. She said, "Hey, everybody, granny has arrived!" She immediately put down what she was holding and ran over to give her grandmother a hug. Dimitri was next, then the girls. Finally, Dani walked over to Nonna and introduced **his** grandmother. "Shimza Duritz, this is my grandmother, Margaret Sandor. Grandma, this is my brother Dushan's great grandmother."

The two ladies grasped hands, then hugged before speaking. Shimza said, "Somehow I feel like we know each other already. So much going on in our families!"

Margaret reached for Shimza's hand again and said, "I feel the same way. It's so nice to finally meet you; Dani speaks very highly of you. I wasn't sure I'd get a chance to meet you."

Introductions done, Dushan turned to Dani and said in a stage whisper, "Watch out my brother, this lady isn't shy about putting idle young men to work."

And Nonna didn't waste any time putting Dani to work, or at least attempting to. As the family sat on the back patio chatting and drinking iced tea, Nonna leaned in close to Dani and said, "Look, I don't mean to impose on you, but the fact that you have a bit of free time on your hands is very fortuitous. I think you'll enjoy what I'm about to suggest." Before responding, Dani looked over at Dushan as if to ask *Is this your doing?* Dushan caught the question, smiled, and resumed his conversation with Margaret.

Dani immediately knew he would enjoy whatever Nonna had in mind. "Your wish is my command. My time is your time, as long as it helps me get to know Liverpool a little better."

"Oh, I think I can guarantee that. You'll get to know the city in a way that even the denizens themselves don't know."

Dani was getting excited at the prospect of being handed a "tour" of Liverpool and the Picton district like none other. "Will it by any chance involve meeting some of your Rom community?"

Nonna smiled and said, "As a matter of fact, yes. Dushan may have told you that I'm going to be teaching 'Sociology of the Rom People' at Liverpool University, right? Well, part of the course will be an introduction to survey research methods, as learned by studying the demographics of the Rom communities. I say 'communities' because there are Rom groups here from several ethnic subgroups. In addition to my students doing some of the surveying, we'll have to have volunteer students from outside the course."

Dani walked over to the dining table, where Nonna had set some materials for a course she would be teaching. He picked up what looked like a syllabus, and glanced through it before turning back to Nonna. "Do you know whether or not your course is open to freshmen? I've signed up for an Intro to Sociology course, but yours would be more interesting, I'm sure."

"I can find out for you; in the past it was only upper classmen who took the course. Perhaps the sociology course you took in high school might count as a prerequisite."

Margaret, who had been listening closely to their conversation, said, "If it would be okay with you, Shimza, I would like to talk with you more about your course. I don't know if Dani told you much about our extended Sandor clan in the UK, but we have a fair number of acquaintances in the different Rom communities. When I get back to Liverpool, may I pay you a visit at the university and discuss your course?"

"Of course! I would love that. I can see that my course is taking shape right before my eyes!"

CHAPTER SIXTEEN:
A FRESHMAN IN LIVERPOOL AND
A CON MAN ON THE LOOSE

Nonna started teaching her course at the beginning of the third week of September 2014. The course began with a couple of overview lectures on Rom history, going back to the 11th century in Turkey and the rest of the Middle East. Margaret gave a guest lecture on the many interwoven connections between the Rom, Greek and Balkan communities, connections that persisted to current times. To nobody's surprise, Nonna was able to finesse permission for Dani to enroll in her course.

As excited as Dani was about the start of the fall semester, a brand-new development in Carolyn's criminal case was making him very nervous. As Carolyn and Derrick Nelson promised back in June at Angus's place, they really put the nail in Bulent Aksoy's coffin with the information they provided to the Liverpool Crown Prosecutor. Or at least that was what everyone thought. With a probation recommendation from the prosecution, and a hopeful, tentative decision from the judge, Carolyn, Margaret, Charlotte and Makelle were pretty sure Carolyn's criminal case would come to an exciting close with Aksoy's arrest and indictment on multiple counts of kidnapping.

And it would have been relatively easy—Derrick had seen Aksoy in a Liverpool casino on several occasions, Derrick being somewhat of a gambling addict. "He looked like he was some kind of pit boss, a supervisor of some blackjack dealers," Derrick told Angus as they had lunch with Dani and Margaret at her home in Liverpool. Angus had seemed to think it would not be too difficult to apprehend Aksoy at work.

Except that Aksoy slipped through the net that Angus and the law enforcement agencies had set around him. Angus wasn't sure how

Aksoy did it, but he was gone. Angus suspected that Aksoy had recognized Derrick in the casino and started making plans for a quick exit if need be.

To their credit, the Crown Prosecutor's office kept its part of the bargain and saw to it that the court affirmed its tentative agreement. Carolyn was a free woman, subject to the six-month jail term she had already served and a five-year probation period that required her to stay within the borders of Her Royal Majesty's realm and obtain meaningful employment working with the rapidly expanding immigrant population. She and everyone else, but especially Dushan's great grandmother Shimza, were looking forward to her imminent future working with Liverpool's social services agency. That exciting future notwithstanding, Carolyn still had some residual fear that Aksoy would some day come looking for her.

Dani refused to believe that Aksoy's escape from justice was the final chapter in this case. *He's not gone; we're gonna find him.* On a hunch, he emailed Dushan to run something by him:

People say Aksoy is gone. Gone is too permanent a word. Folks are scouring the continent looking for the rat. But I'm thinking that since the dude is Turkish, he might feel right at home, and safe, in Turkey, rather than sticking around anywhere in Europe, even in his old haunts in Bosnia. Do you get any vibe about him? Put out your feelers, Dushansky.

Dushan was in his family's new house studying the instructions for assembling the new Ikea computer hutch when his phone chirped with Dani's email. As he read the email, his sister Shimza chuckled and said to him, "Did you even hear what I was saying just now? Can't you put your phone away for a minute?"

Dushan smiled and put his phone on a lampstand. "Sorry, sister dear. Important business from my special agent in Liverpool. He's got an important case he says I have to jump right on. What were you saying?"

Shimza smiled, set down the Isle of Man guidebook she had been perusing, and said, "Well, then, in that case, please forgive me for continuing to talk when you were working a case with your special agent. I was only commenting about some of the interesting hikes in the Douglas area. How is Dani, by the way?"

"Oh, he's fine. Preoccupied with the start of the school year, just like I am. But he just told me that Mr. Bulent Aksoy has flown the coop and must be tracked down, immediately if not sooner. Dani believes the creep's in Turkey somewhere. I don't think so. The political climate in Turkey must be pretty unappealing to a criminal like Aksoy. You remember the email I told you about yesterday from mom and dad's former maid Amina Sidran?"

"You only told me she emailed mom and dad. Did she say something about Turkey?"

"Yeah. She's now running a daycare center in Adana, near the border with Syria. The security apparatus has been rounding up everyone who had any sort of contacts outside the country, or who had lived outside the country. In my book, Mr. Aksoy would be a strong suspect as a corrupting influence on the locals. I'm sure he knew that and would never consider entering Turkey. As soon as I read Dani's text I got a strong hunch that Aksoy had fled anywhere but south. Somewhere out of England's jurisdiction, like maybe Ireland."

Shimza stood up from the chair at the dining table, and walked to the window. After gazing for a few moments at the harbor, she turned to Dushan and said, "I bet Angus would be interested in your theory, even more so if he heard it from both you and Dani. Maybe he'll take a little Irish vacation."

Before getting back to the assembly of the computer hutch, Dushan texted Dani to let him know that he thought Aksoy might be in Ireland. Dushan suggested that Angus might be interested in a nice Irish vacation.

Dani passed along the suggestion to Angus as they were having dinner with Margaret at her place. Angus seemed intrigued. "You know, I was wondering if he might have slipped away to some place more obscure and out of the way than in mainland Europe. I'll look into whether I might be able to interest the Irish authorities into opening an investigation. Of course, they'll probably want to deputise someone with lots of investigative experience."

Dani laughed. "Such as you, perhaps? That's a pretty flimsy excuse for taking an Irish vacation, my friend. But I think you've got a point. You've told us lots of stories of cases you've worked on with the Irish cops."

Margaret laughed as well. "Angus, Angus, Angus, my dear transparent friend. Maybe you need someone to hold your hand if you decide to take that trip. I think I could fulfill that role very well. And I think I would enjoy another visit to Ireland. I never mentioned this before, but I have some distant cousins—or at my age I should say second and third cousins—who live in the Galway area."

Dani smiled and said, "Hey, if you decide to go, can you wait til my midterm break? I'd love to join you. I'm sure Dushan would, too."

Angus chuckled, "Waiting won't be a problem. If we decide to go on this expedition, it won't be for several more months, right Margaret?"

"I'm quite sure it wouldn't be before your fall term is over, Dani. Lots to do and prepare for." Dani wondered what kind of preparation they would need, but that would be fine with him since it would give him time to get through his term at school

Angus stood up and began clearing the dinner dishes. When he returned from the kitchen, he asked Dani, "So, young man, tell us about your school schedule. Did you get into all your classes?"

"Every class but the French class; it was full and I'm on the waiting list. But in the last couple of days, I've started thinking of switching to Manx. After all, my dear brother Dushansky and his sister Shimza tell me they're taking Manx. I've got to keep up with the family. Who needs French, anyway?"

"Whatever you decide. French is a great language to have in your pocket, so to speak. But Manx, I think, would make sense in your circumstances, what with your family living in Douglas. And I doubt the class would fill up; it's one of the more obscure celtic languages. Nevertheless, it is closely related to Irish and Scots-Gaelic. What about your other courses?" Angus asked.

"Geology, Physics, Calculus and History of the Isle of Man."

Margaret said, "Wow, a course on the Isle of Man!" Angus continued, "How interesting. I wonder if it might be possible for me to audit the course. I think I would enjoy it, having grown up and worked there my whole life."

"Well, I can't help you there, but perhaps my well-connected— not to mention persuasive—grandma here can pull some strings. Maybe even suggest you as a guest speaker!" Margaret smiled, winked at Dani, and said, "I'll see what I can do."

*   *   *

102

On the Friday after Dani's term began, he decided to visit a club where the Roman Candles band was playing. He got there early so he could talk to Jaelle some more. He was pleasantly surprised to see Makelle there. Makelle was talking to Jaelle and another woman whom Dani had not seen before. Makelle saw him and introduced him to the woman. "Dani, this is Jaelle's mother, Heike Gewitz." Before Dani could respond, Makelle smiled at Jaelle and said, "I'm trying, Jaelle, but I still haven't got it down."

Dani smiled quizzically as he shook Heike's hand. "Why is Makelle apologizing to your daughter?"

Makelle turned to Dani and said, "I was trying to say 'my daughter Jaelle,' but somehow the words 'my daughter' vanished from my mind before I could say them."

Jaelle chuckled and said to Makelle, "It's quite understandable, 'Pop.' I'll give you a couple more days. But, and this is a big 'but,' you'll have to accomplish that introduction before my band and I leave on our 12-day tour of Europe."

"What!!," said Makelle. "That's fantastic! Where does the tour start?"

"York first, then Edinborough, Dublin, Cork, Paris and Denmark. We should be back home by October 5. I'm trying to talk my mom into coming with us. You should come, too."

Dani said to Jaelle, "Damned inconvenient that it happens so soon after school starts. I'll be up to my eyeballs in course work."

Makelle turned to Heike and asked, "Will you be catching the band on the tour? What's your schedule like?"

"I think I'd like to meet up with the tour in Cork; always wanted to go there, but never have. You should join us there."

Makelle smiled and said, "Sure, why not?" Turning to Jaelle, he asked, "Do you have the date set for the Cork part of the tour?"

"Two nights; September 25th and 26th."

CHAPTER SEVENTEEN:
GETTING COMFY IN DOUGLAS

Dushan and the twins were having a ball in their classes at the Isle of Man University and St. Ninian's. Aisha's favorite teacher at St. Ninian's was Professor Helène Goulet of the French department. She was a French-Canadian woman, mid-thirties, and a former minor consular official at the Dublin Canadian Embassy who had fallen in love with the Isle of Man while on vacation some years earlier. She decided to quit the consular corps and take a teaching job in Douglas rather than endure the two or three-year rotations common in the consular corps. Most of Aisha's classmates in that class were locals, both boys and girls. Her dorm mate, Hana, a Kurdish girl whose family had fled Turkey and settled in Douglas, was in the French class as well. Several of Aisha's male classmates seemed to be particularly smitten with Hana.

Shimza had decided to enroll in a Manx class. Her favorite teacher was Professor Philip Esposito, an American who had spent 20 years teaching Manx at Liverpool University before falling in love with the Isle of Man and "retiring" there. But retirement didn't suit him, so he took a position teaching Manx at St. Ninian's. Professor Esposito was fond of sprinkling personal anecdotes into his lectures on Manx language and history, in particular how he fell in love with Douglas during his first few vacations there.

Dushan's first semester at Isle of Man University was rolling right along. He had decided to major in the pre-law International Relations program, and so far he loved it. His professor in the IR Intro class, Bernie Siegel, was taking a year's sabbatical from Golden Gate University in San Francisco. After class during the second week, Dushan went up to him and asked him if he knew Makelle Ringhiera, another Golden Gate University law professor.

Professor Siegel looked pleasantly surprised and said, "Of course I know him. He's a respected asset of Golden Gate's. I heard he was planning on taking a sabbatical. Did it ever happen?"

"Yes, he just finished the sabbatical; it was at Liverpool University. He's currently working on locating and shutting down some international refugee-smugglers. Makelle told us he decided to take an additional year off from GGU to devote some time combatting the smuggler ring."

"How do you know him?"

"He's a distant relative of my stepbrother Dani, who lives in Liverpool and attends the university there."

Siegel was silent for a few moments, then asked Dushan to join him for a coffee at the student union. They chatted as they walked across the quad to the student union. Siegel pointed to a table near a sunny window and said, "Let's have a seat. I want to hear more about Makelle. Sounds like what he's doing might be something I'd like to get involved in."

About a month into Dushan's first semester, Makelle and Heike arrived to spend a couple of nights with the Sava family, a layover before they would attend Jaelle's band's concerts. Nonna took a week off from her job in Liverpool to tag along. During their visit, they talked Dushan and his sisters into hopping over to Ireland with them to catch Jaelle's gig in Cork at the beginning of the "All Faiths Festival" being held from September 25th through October 4th in an attempt to promote interfaith harmony. The Roman Candles were scheduled to play on the first two days of the Festival, September 25th and 26th. Nonna, Dushan and the girls would accompany Makelle and Heike and catch both days. Marta and Dimitri were too busy at their new jobs to join them.

Because the Jewish holiday of Rosh Hashana fell on Thursday the 25th, their schools would give everyone the following Friday off. The remaining religions honored during that 10-day period were Hindu (Navaratri and Dussehra), Christian (Feast of St. Francis), the second Jewish holiday of Yom Kippur, and the Muslim holiday Eid-al-Adha.

"How come the Roman Candles are playing in a religious music festival," Aisha asked.

"Because a couple of us are Rom and we'll be playing some of the Rom music traditionally played in religious contexts. Don't worry; it's not somber or serious at all. It's basically dance music!"

Just before the Roman Candles' second number in their set began, Dushan whipped out his cell and recorded the song in glorious HD. He immediately emailed the video to Dani, to gloat just a little at being able to see that incredible band in Cork. Dani texted back, *"I'm not amused, Dushansky. But seriously, find out what their, or her, near-term plans are. I'm damned if I'll miss their next gig."*

When the concert was over, Heike and Makelle brought Nonna, Dushan and the twins back stage and introduced them to Jaelle. Makelle said, "This is Dushan, Aisha and Shimza Sava. Do you remember Dani Sandor? Dushan's his stepbrother. This beautiful woman accompanying them is their great grandmother, Shimza Duritz, AKA 'Nonna' to avoid confusion. She works with the Liverpool Rom community, and before that she worked with the Istanbul Rom community."

Jaelle smiled and greeted everyone. "Ms. Duritz, I would love to talk with you more about the Rom community in Liverpool; I know a few of them, being part Rom myself." Turning to Dushan, Jaelle said, "I certainly remember Dani." Turning to Heike and Makelle she said, "What a connection—turns out Dushan's somehow related to you, Makelle!" Turning back to Dushan she asked, "So, do you know the rest of the story of Makelle and my mom and all that?"

"Sure do. Dani and I are pretty close and we keep in touch almost daily."

Aisha and Shimza were speechless for a minute or so, but not Nonna. She didn't hesitate to get into the conversation. She congratulated Jaelle and her bandmates on their set. "It's been quite a while since I've heard such good Rom music. Some of my new friends in the local Rom community can play, but just at home or in the parks and streets busking for tips. They're quite good but they don't have any contacts with the local concert venues yet, but I'm working on that. One of them plays the nyckelharpa, an instrument that would make a great addition to your band."

Jaelle smiled and said, "Thanks. I've seen musicians playing that instrument on YouTube, but never in person. Swedish, I think. Definitely have your friend show up at one of our gigs and maybe we can have him or her sit in. We play a couple of times a week back home in Liverpool; I'll see if I can interest any of our clubs in auditioning some of your Rom musicians. But it'll have to wait til after this tour; we were booked to play gigs in five cities—York,

Edinburgh, Dublin, Cork, Paris and Copenhagen. Paris and Copenhagen are all that are left."

Aisha asked, "And after that, what? Back to Liverpool?"

"Definitely. I need a break; we all need a break. We should be back home on October 5th."

CHAPTER EIGHTEEN:
WHAT ARE THE ODDS

Margaret and Angus were chatting after their dinner with Dani, who was busily checking Facebook and email on his laptop. Thinking he would be ignoring them for the rest of the evening, they were startled when he suddenly shouted, "Oh my God! He's been seen; I knew it!"

"You knew what? Who's been seen?" Margaret and Angus said practically at the same time.

"Aksoy, the slime Bulent Aksoy. Derrick Nelson thinks he saw him in Galway."

Angus set down his tea cup and asked, "Is he sure it was Aksoy?"

"He seems to be. Remember when he saw Aksoy in a casino here? He recognized him then and recognizes him now."

Margaret asked, "Where in Galway? Another casino?"

"Derrick didn't say. I'm gonna reply and ask him. Also I'm gonna let Dushan know."

Angus stood and walked to the little wood stove. It was a cold and rainy late-October day. Turning back to Dani, he said, "Find out if Derrick saw him in a casino and get the name, would you?"

Margaret said, "Angus, dear, is it time to call in that favor you spoke of?"

"What favor," Dani asked, and then turned back to his laptop when it signaled an incoming email. "Okay, Derrick says the creep seemed to be working a card table at the Eglinton Casino in Galway." Turning back to Margaret and Angus, he asked again, "What favor?"

Angus said, "Well, based on the possibility that Aksoy might turn up in Ireland rather than the Continent, I managed to get myself temporarily deputized by the Irish state police to detain 'on reasonable suspicion' the person I've described in my affidavit, Bulent Aksoy."

"Wait, wait, wait," said Dani. "Why would the Irish police give you, Angus, a retired Isle of Man cop, permission to detain an Irish visitor based on what—on suspicion that he's working illegally? Do you know some honcho in Ireland?"

Angus chuckled, "It's funny you should ask. As it happens, I do know someone there, an Irish police officer from Galway. A couple of years before I met Dushan's dad, I had a visit from this young Irish officer who was looking for someone in Douglas, Isle of Man. He was looking for a Turkish criminal who fled there to hide for a while. It wasn't such a hard job for me to find him, since there were very few Turks in Douglas. But the Irish officer thanked me profusely and promised to lend me a hand if I ever needed help in Ireland. He's a big muckety-muck captain now in Galway, and was glad to offer his assistance. So here I am.

"And as to your question about whether Aksoy's working illegally in Ireland, it doesn't matter. That possibility isn't the basis of our probable-cause arrest warrant. What I've alleged in my affidavit is that Aksoy was, and still is, wanted in England for the long-running child-theft scheme he fronted there back in the 90's when Dushan was stolen."

Margaret added, turning to Dani, "And if you haven't guessed already, Angus and I have secured a second star witness to identify the creep if he should be spotted. Our two star witnesses will be none other than my niece Carolyn and her former work colleague Derrick Nelson. They deeply regret the day they met Aksoy and worked with him. Now it's pay back time, we hope."

CHAPTER NINETEEN:
CASINO CAPER

It had been almost two weeks since Bulent Aksoy saw, or thought he saw, Derrick Nelson in the casino. Stifling a rising sense of panic, Aksoy had taken his break from the card table a little early to see if he could follow the man and find out it was indeed Nelson or just someone who looked like Nelson. No luck; the man had disappeared.

After that, Aksoy couldn't decide whether or not he should pull up stakes yet again and find another safe haven, or at least a safer haven than Galway. Trouble was, where to go? After his close call in Liverpool he was sure England and the European continent weren't safe. And Nelson wasn't the only man Aksoy feared would find him. Aksoy's former associates, two French criminals who had been working with him until Aksoy managed to set them up for arrest last year, were probably out of jail by now and would be looking for him.

Aksoy felt frozen; he couldn't make a decision one way or another, whether to stay or figure out where to go. Two weeks passed and he was no closer to deciding what to do. But in the meantime, nothing else had happened, and Aksoy began to be hopeful that he was just being paranoid. Maybe he could get on with his life. *But what kind of life? Do I want to be a blackjack dealer for the rest of my life?* On the other hand, he told himself, it wasn't so bad working at the Eglinton Casino. The pay was decent and Galway was a pretty interesting city.

At the end of his shift, Aksoy decided to have dinner in the casino instead of taking the bus to the Middle Eastern restaurant near his apartment. He finished eating, drank his tea, and paid the check. As the waiter was walking away, Bulent's attention was drawn to a very elegant elderly lady walking into the café. She was so dolled up with fine clothes and jewelry that Bulent hardly noticed the middle-aged bald guy accompanying her. When Bulent got up and started walking out, he got the feeling the bald guy was checking him out. *Probably some faggot,* he chuckled.

Aksoy exited the casino and walked toward the bus terminal a block and a half ahead. It was early yet for the bus he was going to take back to his apartment and it wouldn't be in the terminal yet. He figured he would have to hang out for a few minutes on one of the benches.

When he was just about in the middle of the last block before the terminal plaza, he heard a woman's voice behind him. "Hello! Excuse me! Do you have a moment?"

Aksoy turned around and saw two well-dressed elderly ladies walking toward him. Recognizing one of them, he said to her, "Oh, hello. Didn't I just see you a few minutes ago in the casino café? What can I do for you?"

Shimza spoke up, "Yes, and I thought I recognized you so I tried to follow you."

Aksoy chuckled. "Well, you've caught me. As I said, what can I do for you?"

"My name is Shimza, and this is my dear friend, Margaret. When I saw you in the café, I instantly recognized you. Margaret was already in the café, and she wanted to meet you as well."

"Meet me? And you say you recognized me; from where and when?" He was developing a headache and starting to feel dizzy. He took a deep breath and said to the ladies, "Do you mind if we have a seat on this bench here? I need to sit for a moment. Now, tell me how you know me."

Shimza said, "Margaret and I want to thank you for finding—at least indirectly—a home and family for a boy – now a wonderful young man – who was taken from my granddaughter and her husband some 15 years ago."

Aksoy was as stunned as he was puzzled. Some unrecognizable feeling was creeping up on him. He had no idea what to say or do, except to shake hands with each woman. But that only made his dizziness worse.

Margaret said, "It was my son's family that adopted the boy, Dushan. He grew up in California with my grandson, Dani. I don't think you ever met Dushan, but the two stepbrothers are enjoying their semester break from their colleges, one in Douglas, Isle of Man, and one in Liverpool. Dani just flew in from Liverpool to visit Dushan, who's vacationing here in Galway with his family. We were on our way to meet them at the transit terminal."

Aksoy was getting more uncomfortable by the minute. Something about the story these two were telling him didn't make sense, and yet it reminded him of what he used to do when he lived in England, facilitating "adoptions." Addressing Shimza, he asked, "You say your granddaughter's son was taken and raised by another family. I'm afraid I don't understand why you say you recognize me. When did this happen, and where?" Aksoy's throat felt parched, he was swallowing a lot, and he was getting very agitated.

Shimza stood up at the sound of approaching footsteps. "I think I see my great grandson, his father and stepbrother coming. I'll let them explain how that happened."

Dimitri, Dushan and Dani walked toward the three of them, and Shimza said to Dimitri, "Dimitri, I was just about to answer this gentleman's question about how Dushan was abducted."

Dimitri said to Aksoy, "I'm Dushan's father." Pointing to Dushan he said, "This is my son." Pointing to Dani, he said, "This is my son's stepbrother, Margaret's grandson, Danilo. Actually, the three of us are not the best ones to answer your question. Dani's parents might have been able to clarify the situation, but they've long since passed away. Dani's aunt would be the one with the whole story. She and her former colleague, it just so happens, are here on holiday and met Dani, Dushan and me this very morning. I think they're coming up now."

Before Aksoy could stand and greet them, his feeling of lightheadedness increased so much that he thought he might faint if he stood. His heart was racing, but he still didn't know why this man, and the ladies, were telling him all this. What did the story have to do with him?

The woman whom Dimitri called Dani's aunt walked up and spoke first. "I think I can answer the question you're probably asking yourself, Bulent. But first, let me introduce myself." Extending her hand to him, this vaguely familiar woman said, "I'm Carolyn Owen, from way back in your past. Isle of Man? Liverpool? Does either place ring a bell?"

Before Carolyn had finished speaking, Bulent almost choked on the words "Isle of Man." When Derrick stepped forward and smiled,

Bulent recognized him and had had enough. He jumped up from the bench like a jackrabbit surprised by a coyote. He sprang forward but stopped abruptly. The others in the group were now forming a semicircle in front of him. He spun around to run the other way, but two very burly men stood in his way—Angus and his Irish counterpart.

The Irish police officer stepped forward and spoke, "These people have identified you as Bulent Aksoy. According to my documents here, you are a Turkish citizen who recently moved to Ireland after several decades living in Britain. There is a warrant for your arrest issued out of Liverpool, which I am serving on you at this time."

The officer approached Aksoy, who turned and bolted in the other direction. Rather than plow through the group of men and women facing him, he swerved to the right toward the sidewalk. Carolyn and Dimitri peeled off from the group and raced ahead of him. Bulent charged right at Carolyn, as a bull at a bullfighter. But like any good bullfighter, Carolyn stepped aside at the last minute, pivoted to her left and grabbed Aksoy's shirt collar as he attempted to run past her. Using Aksoy's momentum, Carolyn pulled him to the left, causing him to lose his balance and crash into Dimitri. Before he could recover his balance, Dimitri threw him to the ground, sat on his back and pulled Aksoy's arms behind him. The others encircled Aksoy as the police officer handcuffed him.

CHAPTER TWENTY:
REUNION

Aisha and Shimza were not used to the limelight they were in yesterday at school. Last week, when their professors Goulet and Esposito heard about their family's capture of the notorious criminal Bulent Aksoy over in Galway, they arranged for the girls to introduce their brothers to an assembly at St. Ninian's. Everyone in the school—not to mention the whole of Douglas—had read or heard about the capture. Dani had taken a couple of days off from classes at Liverpool University and come over at the school's invitation to be a co-presenter along with Dushan and his sisters. The school also invited the two women who had masterminded the whole capture—Margaret and Shimza.

The event went well, and gave a considerable boost to the girls' popularity afterwards. Now it was Friday afternoon in the Sava household in Douglas. The whole gang was there—not just the Savas and Dani, but Nonna, Angus, Margaret, Carolyn, Derrick, Charlotte, Makelle, Jaleh and Tom.

Dani's phone rang and he put it on speaker. "Hello, Claude. Where are you?"

"You won't believe this, but I just arrived in Liverpool to pay you a visit, but you're not at home. Where are you?"

Aisha whispered to Margaret, "Is that the Claude that Dani saved last year in the Utah mountains?"

Margaret answered, "Yes, one and the same. Maybe we'll get to meet him."

Claude's voice came back over the phone, "Guess who I have with me? Two old friends of your brother's mom, Milan Vukadin and Jovan Durkovic."

Marta immediately jumped up and moved over to be nearer to

Dani's phone. She practically shouted into it, "Claude, hi, I'm Marta, Dani's 'stepmom,' so to speak. I'm Dushan's biological mom. We have a surprise for you, a big surprise. But you'll have to come over here to find out what it is."

"Where is 'here,' Marta? Are you not in Liverpool?"

Dani said, "Claude, we're all in Douglas, Isle of Man, just across the Irish Sea from Liverpool, where Dushan's family now lives. You've got to come over, man. Catch the Isle of Man Steam Packet ASAP and call me when you arrive. Can you come today?"

"Probably not tonight, but yes, tomorrow morning. Can't wait to see you again. And Jovan and Milan I'm sure will want to reunite with your family. I'll call you in the morning."

Dani grinned and looked at everyone as he said into the phone, "Great! The party will be complete."

Dimitri, getting up from the couch after Dani ended the call, said, "And this amazing story will be complete, perhaps."

"Perhaps, yes. Perhaps is the operative word," Dushan said as he reached for Dani's phone.